Angeline Teal

John Thorn's Folks

A Study of Western Life

Angeline Teal

John Thorn's Folks
A Study of Western Life

ISBN/EAN: 9783744766845

Printed in Europe, USA, Canada, Australia, Japan

Cover: Foto ©Andreas Hilbeck / pixelio.de

More available books at **www.hansebooks.com**

John Thorn's Folks

A

Study of Western Life

BY

ANGELINE TEAL

BOSTON
LEE AND SHEPARD PUBLISHERS
NEW YORK CHARLES T. DILLINGHAM
1884

ELECTROTYPED BY
C. J. PETERS AND SON, BOSTON.

JOHN THORN'S FOLKS.

——◆——

CHAPTER I.

THE Kitzmillers were new-comers in the Wycoff settlement. They had left a pleasant home in a State farther east, and taken up their abode in this comparatively new region, for the simple mathematical reason that the price of a small farm of rather thin land there would purchase a large one of very rich land here.

The family consisted of the united head, and two children: Leander, aged twenty-one, just the commonplace rural young man, and Olive, not commonplace at all, but a lovely, dark-skinned child of eighteen, with feelings as ardent as August sunshine, and pure as dew.

The house before which the canvas-covered flitting-wagons stopped, one day in the early spring, was a long, low frame structure, with

1

verandahs running the entire length, both in front
and rear. It was one of the ten or dozen frame
houses which the township, exclusive of the
village of New Madrid, could boast. The
house was quite new. There were capacious
log stables and out-buildings, and an orchard
of thrifty young fruit-trees, not yet come into
bearing. The original owner of the place had
been constrained to sell it, under pressure of
sorrow and discouragement. His wife had died,
leaving him with a brood of little ones on his
hands. Friends at the east offered help with
the children if he would return there, and Mr.
Kitzmiller appearing at this juncture and offering an honest price, the farm became his.

It was called an improved farm, though on
half the land the heavy timber stood untouched,
and the remainder was thickly studded with
stumps, too green for lifting. Kitzmiller and
his wife were well pleased with the change
they had made. It would prove a wise one in
the long run, and the "long run" was what
these people always considered. They were
essentially industrious and patient, and their
son, inheriting largely these qualities of his
parents, was also well satisfied with the new

home. To own a goodly number of these inex-
haustible acres ; to build a house and people it
with a family of his own ; to raise stock and
watch the growth of such lush crops as the
inky soil produced, such were the calm and
reasonable ambitions of his heart. A school-
section cornered upon his father's land, which
could be bought cheaply. It was covered with
virgin forest, the great tree-boles of walnut and
poplar standing so thick that a deer could only
traverse it with antlers held oblique. Young
Kitzmiller scarcely thought of the millions of
axe-strokes it would require to bring that land
under cultivation, but he did think of the
time, not far distant, when the coming of the
portable sawmill and the railroad would turn
that forest into a gold-mine.

It was a land of promise, if not of present
beauty. Little Olive cared not for the promise,
while the newness and wildness filled her, at
first, with a pitiful homesick longing. She
had been reared on the spot where she was
born, and her life had been very bright and
simple. Her feelings after the removal may
have been something like those of a household
pet suddenly encaged in a bosky wilderness.

But the setting to rights of the new house afforded her a keen pleasure.

There was a corner cupboard in the sitting-room, and in this she arranged her mother's set of blue and white Liverpool ware, not a piece of which had been broken in the transit. In another corner of the same large room a white-wood book-case was erected, and on it she placed the miscellaneous assortment of volumes that constituted their small library. There were a good many school-books, and some Patent-Office Reports, all utilized with a view to filling space and magnifying the appearance of the collection. Scott's Infantry Tactics found a niche between Don Quixote and an odd volume of Macaulay's Essays; and Barrington's Sketches shouldered McCosh on the Divine Government. The remainder of that shelf, after McCosh, was filled with books of a similar tone, — McCheyne's Sermons, the Pilgrim's Progress, the works of Doddridge, Boston, and Baxter.

Olive's eyes rested upon this row of serious books with an interest she could not have explained. She had never read them; but were they not the tables of the law? and would not the tabernacle that contained them be under sacred protection? The feeling of security was deepened when, on the Sunday morning after their arrival, she knelt with parents and brother, while the good farmer asked the Divine blessing in the same set phrases she had listened to from infancy. The family altar made the new place home.

In due time the Kitzmillers made the acquaintance of their neighbors. The first step in this direction was the formal entertaining of a visiting party. Mr. Henry Wycoff, passing the house one day on his way to New Madrid, halted and informed Mrs. Kitzmiller that she might expect company on the next day but one. His mother and his wife and a few other women, supposing them to be about settled, had concluded to make them a call. Mrs. Kitzmiller knew very well what a "call," in country parlance, signifies; she was used to this mode of testing a new neighbor's hospitality, and set about with pleased alacrity to boil her most savory ham, and produce her whitest loaves for the occasion. There was also a browning of richly-flavored coffee, and a stewing of home-dried peaches, till all the region around was saluted by delicious odors.

They came early, and spent the day, — old Mrs. Wycoff, young Mrs. Wycoff, and four other leading ladies of the neighborhood. The elder Mrs. Wycoff introduced herself and her friends to Mrs. Kitzmiller, who received them with frank friendliness, and helped them off with their things, while Olive stood ready to carry bonnets and shawls and deposit them on her mother's curtained bed. Then there were a couple of babies to be unrolled and generally attended to, and these small objects of universal feminine interest drew the hearts of hostess and guests together, and unsealed a tide of genial talk, which diverged into innumerable channels, but knew no slack or ebb till the declining sun warned the good women that milking-time was near, and the newly-weaned calves were bleating at their empty troughs.

Through this all-day visitation, the new people were made acquainted, not only with the six families represented, but with the neighborhood in general, and "John Thorn's folks" in particular.

When the Thorns were mentioned Mrs. Kitzmiller and Olive listened with quickened interest, for the reason that they were their nearest neighbors, and that there seemed to be something eccentric about the people and their way of living. The two houses were in full view of each other, and Olive, in her lookings that way, had observed that the stated performances of farm-house life did not go on there in the ordinary manner. For instance, there was no regular Monday's washing, but a few clothes were hung out almost any day of the week, sometimes even on Sunday. There were other signs of mismanagement and desultoriness at the house, all in strong contrast to the well-appointed farm and tannery, for Thorn was a tanner as well as a farmer.

"I wish you had brought Mrs. Thorn with you to-day," said Mrs. Kitzmiller. "We are such near neighbors, we ought to become acquainted."

"Ten to one you won't be for the next two years, unless some favorin' accident should happen," said Mrs. Wycoff, senior. "As for askin' her to come with us visitin', I'd as soon 'a' thought of askin' old Bloodroot. She's a medicine squaw, that lives down by Half-Moon Lake. Miss Thorn is odder'n odd!"

Following this climax came a history of the

Thorns, given in a somewhat scattering manner by the different members of the company. The reader shall be favored with a more consecutive one.

CHAPTER II.

SOME years before, an old Scotchman named Ludlow had settled upon a tract of wild land in New Madrid township. His family at first comprised a wife, a son, and a daughter; but within a year or two after their coming the boy and his mother both died, leaving the old man with his daughter Emily as his sole companion and housekeeper. Ludlow had been a cloth-draper in Scotland, and had come to America with the intention of investing his savings in western lands. That he had brought with him a hoard of some bulk none of his neighbors at first doubted. Among them its estimate varied from a few hundred dollars to some tens of thousands. After a while, however, the belief in his riches gradually faded out of the public mind; he bought no more land; he loaned no cash to any one, though frequently applied to by responsible parties, who offered him fair interest. His energies seemed prostrated by the loss of his wife and son, and a year after the death of the latter he was stricken

with paralysis and carried into his cabin a helpless cripple for life.

Emily Ludlow was a trifle past fourteen years
old when her mother died, leaving her to a
most forlorn and miserable existence. Her
father was severe to cruelty; he was also miser-
ly to the last degree, and forced her to subsist
on the coarsest food and wear only such garments as she could fashion from the wardrobe
of her dead mother. He welcomed no one to
his door, and rudely repulsed one kind woman
who visited the house with offers of sympathy
and help to the poor child. After he was
palsied Emily planted and hoed in the field as
usual, running in to wait upon her father when
he pounded on the window-sash with his cane.
She generally managed to keep out of reach of
his ill-aimed blows, and to his curses and com-
plaints she grew hardened. They were left in
time quite to themselves, no one going near
them save John Thorn.

He happened to be passing near Ludlow's
cabin on the day of the latter's paralytic seizure.
Emily, running out for help, met him a few
rods from the house; he went with her and
carried her father from the clearing, where he

had fallen, in to his bed, and called every day for a week till the old man was able to sit up and give his orders in partly intelligible language. He came afterwards from time to time and performed many little commissions for the invalid, such as bringing his tea and tobacco from the village store, and procuring him canes and crutches of various styles, none of which served him for any other use than pounding on the floor and shaking at the head of poor Emily. He was a wrathful, bad old man in those helpless days. Possibly his unaccountable rages, followed by long seasons of the deepest gloom, may have been in part due to the fact that he suffered horribly from hepatic engorgement. One can readily understand how it happens that in New England, where people exist in blissful unconsciousness of their livers, they find it difficult to accept original sin, total depravity. and various other depressing doctrines that come quite natural to the inhabitants of malarial regions, particularly when the autumns are moist and warm.

John Thorn frequently saw Ludlow in his worst tempers, and the fact that he seemed to derive amusement from his impotent oaths and grumblings caused Emily to conceive a strong aversion to him. His acts were always kind, yet she grew to look upon him as one who could laugh at suffering, who knew no pity, who in his cold indifference to her humiliating trials was as much more cruel than her father as he was younger and stronger.

"I wish you would never come here again!" she cried passionately one day, when he had laughed at her confused attempts to follow her father's contradictory directions about preparing and serving his dinner; "I can do for my father alone, and you only come here to jeer at us and tell other people how badly we get on!"

To this John laughingly replied by advising her to get a new dog, and a very cross one, as he was not at all afraid of old Tinker.

Thorn had been a resident of the county a few years longer than the Ludlows. He was a bachelor of thirty, and his domestic affairs were presided over by a deaf old woman whom he called Aunt Thirsa. He once told Jared Wycoff how this queer personage came to be his housekeeper. His mother died when was a child, and Thirsa Winchel, a distant relative and a childless widow, took temporary charge of his father's household. His father married again; other children came; John was crowded harder and harder till he left home, partly driven out, partly frozen out. Winchel stayed on, always with a stocking to darn or a child to tend. John's father gave him some money, with which he went to school for a year or two. Then he hired with a tanner, learned the trade rapidly, and soon earned good wages. At the age of twenty-three he had saved enough to buy land in Indiana. He went home one day to say good-bye, and found Aunt Thirsa in great distress. The hard second wife was about sending her to the poor-house.

"I could earn my living still," moaned the poor creature, "if some one would find me a place to work where I would n't have to learn new things!"

John begged another night's lodging for her under the old roof, then took her with him to the West, and installed her as general mis-manager of his new home. No stronger proof could a man give of innate kindliness of disposition than Thorn gave by his unfailing patience with old Thirsa; for he endured much discomfort which might have been bettered had it so pleased the dull, slow, obstinate dependent, who would brook neither help nor helpful suggestion. Yet he was held by people about him to be a strong, shrewd man, capable in many directions, yet less capable of gentleness to his kind than most others. He was respected, but scarcely liked. Country maidens and young widows cast admiring glances at his fine figure and superb horsemanship; but when they noted that he rode with a bit that drew blood, and heard about his shooting a valuable bull for breaking a fence and leading the herd into a wheatfield, they shook their prudent heads and commiserated the possible wife of such a husband. Through all his unloved childhood and youth he had hardly thought of pitying himself, and his persistent effort to make light of his own buffetings had fixed upon him a habit of mind that made it possible for him to shock the feelings of those accustomed to the ordinary and understandable expressions of human sympathy. Without there was a crust of terse formality, of offensive indifference; within was a heart of fire, but no one suspected it, not even John Thorn.

CHAPTER III.

SOME twenty months after the first, Ludlow had another shock of palsy. It was a light one, but left him very much prostrated. The day following, Thorn called at the cabin, remained awhile within, then went out to where Emily was busily hoeing in the corn-field.

"Stop your work awhile, Emily," he said, with a new gravity and gentleness in his voice. "I want to talk with you."

She obeyed, letting the hoe fall at her feet, and folding her arms to rest them while she listened.

"Your father is going to die. The end will come in a week or two at farthest. You will be left quite alone then, and I would like to make you my wife before he goes. He seems to wish it, and I have for a long time wished it."

"Your wife!" she almost screamed. "I hate you, John Thorn, and you know it! I would hide myself and die in the woods first!"

She was a tall girl of seventeen now, and

very lovely. She straightened herself proudly, throwing back the rich chestnut hair from a forehead whose whiteness no sun or wind could stain, and looked at him in pale defiance. Thorn smiled slightly as he said, —

"That is about the kind of answer I expected, and some progress has been made. I am coming back to-morrow, and you will, maybe, talk differently then, or be silent, which will amount to consent; for, look here, my violent child, I am going to make you such pledges as no other man ever made the girl he liked and wanted for his own. You shall have the most absolute liberty in everything — to go where you please, do what you like, — my watch over you amounting only to necessary protection. Until you desire my love it shall never be thrust upon you. No requirements of any sort shall be placed upon you; you are to be left sole mistress of your own movements and your own time, and, unless you choose to do so, you need never spend an hour alone with me, making allowance for unavoidable accidents. Think of it till to-morrow," and he was gone.

The next day he again found Emily hoeing.

"Why do you work so hard?" he asked;

"you know you will leave this place in a few days."

For a minute she stood silent with her eyes on the ground; then looked up and said:

"I never told a lie in my life, not even to save myself a beating. If I thought"— she hesitated and looked down.

"If you thought I would keep my pledges, you mean," said Thorn. "I am not a liar, either, Emily. I always have this handy," showing the hilt of a revolver, "and I would put a ball through my head sooner than have you taunt me with breaking them. You are safe enough." He waited a little for her to speak; she did not, and he said:

"You'll go home with me, then, when he does n't need you any longer?"

Still she was silent.

"All right," said Thorn briefly, and turned away.

She watched him as he strode across the clearing, noting for the first time in her life his erect carriage, the fine poise of his head, and the wonderful energy of all his movements. She recalled a remark made by her father in one of his rare moods of talkativeness,—"He'll

be a great man in these parts one day, will Jack
Thorn."

"I wonder why he wants me," she said to
herself; she fell to musing and worked no more
that day.

Returning from a walk, one afternoon a few
days later, Emily found Thorn in the house,
and with him another man. Jared Wycoff was
the eldest son of the house of Wycoff, which
was one of the oldest in the county. When a
youth he had been racked with ague and dosed
with calomel, till the mercurial poison, in its
contest with the malarial poison, had twisted his
spine and hips, deforming and laming him for
life. He had spent some years in an eastern
State, pursuing his studies while being under
medical treatment. When he returned to Indiana he was installed as winter schoolmaster
for life, made a justice of the peace, and en-
dowed with most of the other small offices in
the gift of the good people among whom he
lived.

When Emily entered, Jared sat figuring upon
some official blanks, a tin case on his knee serving him for a desk. The poor, lame fellow had
been making one of his rounds as township

assessor; he was very tired and in a hurry to get home, so Thorn said:

"Squire Wycoff has called to marry us, Emily. I have the license here; if you are ready we will not keep him waiting."

She hesitated a moment, while a soft, pink flush suffused cheek, neck, and brow; then she reached him the hand that was nearest him, as they stood. It chanced to be the left one; Thorn took it quickly and held it in both his own, while the Justice in few words made them husband and wife.

The two men went away together. Late that evening a good-natured, red-headed boy made his appearance at Ludlow's. He said his name was Davy Ransom; he lived on John Thorn's place, and Thorn had sent him to "stay around" a few days, as Emily might not like to be alone when her father was so bad.

Thorn himself did not return for two days. On the morning of the third, old Ludlow began to worry over his absence and desired Emily to send for him. This she declined to do, or at least put him off; whereupon he upbraided her for a "stubborn wench," and accused her of affronting a husband who was too good for her.

In the afternoon he seemed all at once to grow weaker, and as he still continued to wish that " Jack " would come, Emily was on the point of sending Davy Ransom for him when Thorn entered the door. Emily blushed again, that delicate, wild-rose blush, and drooped her eyelids beneath the warm, sweet smile with which he greeted her.

"Send the lad away," said the old man with an air of haste ; "yes, and the gell, too."

Davy went out and began chopping at the woodpile. Emily sat still, and her father did not seem to mind her. Motioning Thorn to come near the bedside the old Scot said in a low, eager tone :

"It's i' the auld tree, Jack ! Can ye see the little honey-locust at the fut o' the clearin'? Gae doon to thot, then tak twa hunnerd gude steps stret east, thro the thick timmer. Ye'll find yersel near a big tulip-tree, wi' a hole in its side. Gae on ye knees and peer oop at the dure o' the tree. Ye'll see some'at ; bring it me quick."

John went out, and bidding Davy follow him, steered straight for the big tree. Emily sprang to the window ; she observed that he did not follow directions by going down to the honey-locust and counting his steps from there, but went direct and unhesitating from the cabin door. The fact was, he knew the old tulip tree by sight, as he did many other ancient trees in the region, and did not need landmarks to find it. Stooping at the aperture and looking up, his eye caught a glint of something bright, about eight feet from the ground. Davy introduced his body into the hollow of the tree without difficulty and elbowed his way a short distance up its sides; then bracing back and knees, reached down a covered tin-pail of some size.

After he had emerged, covered with red dust and debris, and John had taken the pail, they both stood and looked curiously at the old tree. A light breeze stirring its top caused it to tremble ominously on its spongy sap-ring.

"What a shaller dodge that wus!" said the boy. "A sand-hill crane 'd know'd better 'n to built her nest in that old shell. Any stiff blow mought 'a' flopped it over 'n then some gump like me 'd found the cash!"

John did not open the tin treasure casket till he reached the old man's bedside; then in

Emily's presence — Davy having been dismissed at the wood-pile — he counted the contents of the pail, some three thousand dollars, mostly in gold coin, with a few bank-notes, the latter sewed in buckskin and very mouldy.

"Tak it all, Jack," said Ludlow, "and wi' its holp mak o' yersel a rich mon. It was meant for my ain laid, as is gone afore me; now it's yours. Ye'll do fairly by the gell I ken, and a woman's na gude wi' money till her hond."

He lived yet a week longer. Old Mrs. Wycoff and other kind neighbors appeared upon the scene, and assisted Emily in her nursing and watching. John Thorn came and went; but Emily blushed no more at his coming. She mused about him no more in his absence, nor asked herself again, "Why does he want me?" She thought she knew; it was for the money. He had known of its existence, and to make himself legally sure of it had first made sure of her. Her mental journey to this conclusion was a very short one. Undoubtedly his designs upon her father's gold were at the bottom of all his neighborly attentions to them as a family, and prompted that last extraordinary step with reference to herself. Believing this, she straightway proceeded to lavish upon him, in her heart, that choice and racy scorn which we all feel to be the rightful due of selfish and mercenary beings who hold us in their power. Nevertheless, she went home with him after her father was buried.

She was introduced to Aunt Thirsa with much difficulty. John shouted the name Emily very loud in the old woman's best ear; but he did not call her *wife*. Her father had died, and she was going to live with them now; this was all the explanation he gave of her coming. Old Thirsa was so nearly stone deaf that no voice but John's could make her hear, and she paid but little heed to the visible language of motion going on about her; so it may be considered doubtful whether the fact of Emily's existence, to say nothing of her marriage to Thorn, had ever reached her knowledge. She kept on sifting yellow meal through her fingers into the great kettle of "suppawn" she was stirring over the fire; but the smile that accompanied her nod of welcome was neither meaningless nor unkind.

"Try and feel at home, Emily," John said briefly. "Make Aunt Thirsa understand, if you can, what you would like for your meals; possibly you may have to show her how to cook it. I must go now. I started a drove of cattle south a week ago. One of the men came back yesterday, and tells me they are herded in a field near Stone's Crossing, and the river is so high they can't ford. I am going to help drive them east to the old French road. Good-by."

CHAPTER IV.

HE was gone a month. During that month Emily found plenty of time to plan the routine of her life. A part of a day sufficed for setting in order the whitewashed chamber assigned her as her own. Then she tried to help the old housekeeper, but all attempts in that direction were firmly put down. Thirsa needed no help, and would have none, and, while life and the power of resistance lasted, would brook no interference and no innovations. There were corn-cakes, ham or bacon, and coffee for breakfast; boiled meat and vegetables for dinner; suppawn and sweet milk for supper. A couple of quiet, stolid farm hands sat down regularly to the table. Sometimes Emily took her meals with them, sometimes alone. She was allowed to do her own washing and ironing. The family washing was done at sundry times and in divers manners, as were also the churning, bread-making, soap-boiling, &c.

Having little to do indoors, Emily roamed abroad, making the acquaintance of many a wild and lovely nook, with the sure aptitude of one whose love of nature is a birth-gift. She explored Thorn's farm with deep interest. There were strong, dark fields, slowly maturing their crops of wheat and corn. There were acres of level meadow, waving with red-top and timothy, that had been reclaimed by drainage from the wildest swamp. And beyond the meadows lay a stretch of heavy timber that on one side thinned away into breezy oak-openings.

" He was rich enough before," thought Emily ; " yet how much he must have wanted that bit of money ! "

Then she wandered down to the tannery on the brook. There was a long frame building in which Bayless, the currier, worked. There was also a small cabin a few rods distant, where the currier lived with his wife and children. Davy Ransom lived with them, having no relatives of his own. The tan-pits were enclosed by a strong fence and a locked gate, and beyond the pit-yard was the bark-shed, containing a vast pile of oak bark — cords upon cords of it, stacked up to dry. Beside the shed was the bark-mill, and in it she found Davy Ramson, and was glad to find him; she wanted to hear some one talk, and Davy was quite willing to accommodate her.

"He's a first-rate tanner, John Thorn is, but he don't work much in the curryin' shop now; don't have no time. Don't have no time to farm it much, either. Funny thing when a feller's got so much to do he can't do nothin'. John's a mighty good boss, though; keeps the best of tools, and everything handy. He buys hides and sells leather, and, since Truesdale's been around, he's taken to buyin' cattle and drovin' 'em east. He bought his first drove of Truesdale. The woods is all alive with cattle, and Truesdale takes 'em for swamp land. Some of Truesdale's folks got holt of most a hull township of wet land onct. They lived 'way off in York State and never see the land, ony a sharkin' agent put it onto 'em. It was willed to Truesdale, and he's been out here, livin' down to New Madrid, sellin' of it off. The county's ditched, part of it, and he sells sharp, and they say he's goin' to get rich out of it yet. He takes lots of cattle for pay. The woods is just alive with cattle 'round here. They gets mired, and trees fall on 'em, and the rattlers bite 'em, and then off comes their hides off, 'n John Thorn buys 'em, for a chew of plug, so t' speak, and chucks 'em in them ole vats. That's the way *he* gets his money back. They're a hull team — Thorn and Truesdale — and a brindle dog under the wagon."

The bark-mill was under a large circular shed. The axle of the drive-wheel was a vertical shaft reaching from the floor to a cross-beam under the roof. From a joint on this shaft, something higher than a tall man's head, a long arm or sweep extended, dipping slightly downward, till the strap at its end could be attached to the harness of a fat old horse, which plodded around a smooth track, with the contemplative air of a studious person walking for exercise. It was Davy's work to break up the strips of dry bark over the edge of the iron hopper, while old Charley's deliberate promenade ground it to the required fineness.

"I like that work of yours," said Emily; "I believe I could do it."

"I'll bet you could. Want to try?"

"Yes."

Davy stood aside, and Emily took the light wooden mallet and slowly chipped the brittle bark, watching it fall among the rusty cog-wheels. Presently she said,

"Whenever I feel like doing anything, I intend to come down here and grind bark."

When Thorn returned, he approached his home by way of the tannery. He rode quite close to the bark-mill and surprised Emily at her novel employment.

"Why do you do that?" he demanded.

"Because I want to," she replied. "I like it. I intend to grind bark a great deal, but Davy must always stay close by, to carry the strips from the shed, and take it off my hands when I get tired."

"All right," said the master of the place; "you may grind all the bark in the shed, if it pleases you." And he rode on to the house.

Thorn had accompanied his drove to the State line mainly for the sake of giving Emily a little time in which to become used to her new surroundings, unembarrassed by his presence. He wanted time to think things over, too, and he could always think best on horseback.

He had loved the beautiful Scotch girl for a long time; he could not distinctly recall the first beginning. When he became aware that all

the zest of action, all the sweetness of living
had its spring in the thought of her, he remembered, also, that he had unfortunately secured
her bitter aversion. He took no steps to over-
come this, because he did not know what steps
to take. When he saw that her father's end
was near, he followed an impulse and secured
her to himself, with the hope that in the sun of
his unfailing kindness, the snows of her dislike
would one day melt, carrying away, as with a
spring flood, the strange barriers between them.
On that long, solitary homeward ride, John
asked himself why it was that this hope was
so near dead, that it lay on his soul with a
bitter weight. Emily had given him no volun-
tary sign that she was ever any nearer to him
than now; yet he felt sure that once, for a
few days, she had been nearer. He could
recall nothing but that faint color-change,
which had twice marked his approach. Yes,
and that day when she gave him her hand before the justice, it had lain with a soft willingness in his, which it thrilled him to remember.
Then came the counting of that money at her
father's bedside. When he next scanned her
face it had hardened into the look of quiet scorn

which it had worn ever since. He readily divined the process of her thought, and he chafed bitterly over the disadvantage at which she held him. For the present there was nothing to be done, he thought, only to give his captive the length of a long tether.

"If I could see her have some joyous, carefree, girlish years, I would be content."

So spoke the good angel in him.

"At all events I shall not be slain by ever seeing her the wife of another."

Thus spoke the man. And——.

"I will keep and hold her fast, till death parts us, though we are never aught but a blight and a curse to each other!"

Thus the demon. The three contended for the mastery within him over all those miles of forest and open country, till he reached his home, worn out in body and spirit.

A day or two after his return, Thorn met Emily coming out of the gate with a bundle in her arms.

"Where may you be going, and what have you there?" he smilingly asked.

She opened one end of her package and showed him the contents,—a set of fine, small-figured chintz bed-curtains, that had been her mother's.

"I am going to Squire Wycoff's. His wife is going to help me make a dress out of this stuff. She was here the other day."

"You can have new stuff for dresses, Emily, as many as you wish," said John.

"But I like this; it will be pretty."

She was about passing him, but he stopped her in the gateway and said gently,

"I wish, Emily, you would let me buy you something handsome to wear; a new gown — anything you might like."

"Thank you, sir; but I can get my own things," she answered, with a flash of childish petulance. "I am not quite poverty-stricken. I believe my father left me the land; it shall be sold, so that I can have money for clothes and books. I intend to read a good deal."

John still barred the gateway.

"That money, Emily, out of the old tree — I wish the lightning had struck it! — I will pour it in your lap this hour, if you will take it. It is rightfully yours."

"It is not mine, and I would not touch it."

"I will sink it in the lake, or bury it in the

earth, so deep that no man can ever see it again, if you will only trust me — try to like me a little."

She gave him one quick startled look, then cast a glance around, as if seeking some pathway of escape. He moved aside from the gate, and she passed out with rapid steps and averted face.

For some distance she walked rapidly, with her mind in a state of strong agitation ; but this feeling presently passed away. Her inward rage over the mean advantage she supposed Thorn to have taken of her when he hurried her into marriage had subsided during the weeks of his absence; and her dislike was as quiet, if a little deeper, than formerly. He had certainly improved her situation by bringing her to his house on the hill, from which she could have an airy view of more cleared space than from any other point in many miles. She liked these glimpses of airy distance as well as she liked the depths of forest gloom in which she could lose herself whenever she wished. Simply to go where she pleased, do what she pleased, as John had promised, was all she at present desired. It was glorious liberty after many months of bondage. She did not fear that he

would lay constraint upon her or violate his
word.   He was no promise-breaker; she somehow felt secure in that.   And her life had been
too solitary; she was altogether too untaught to
understand the unnaturalness of her position in
Thorn's house.

She spent several days at Mr. Wycoff's house.
The schoolmaster was at home and talked with
her a good deal.   He seemed to be studying
her.   To his wife, Emily was a puzzle.   One
day the affectionate Katy went up to her as she
sat sewing, and kissed her cheek.

"Why did you do that?" asked the girl
blankly.

"Because I felt like it," responded Mrs.
Wycoff.   "Is it possible you were never kissed
in your life before!"

Emily thought a moment, and said calmly,

"I believe I never was; not that I remember."

From Jared, Katy received instructions not
to talk much about Mr. Thorn, and not to mani-
fest the slightest feminine curiosity about this
strange young bride's emotions.

"She is nothing but a beautiful grown-up
child," he said.

CHAPTER V.

"SHE never works, as anybody knows of," said old Mrs. Wycoff on the occasion of that first visit at Mrs. Kitzmiller's; "only to fool 'round the bark-mill once in a while, pretendin' to help grind bark. Yes, and she sews a little, but Jared's wife makes all her dresses."

"Land knows they 're plain enough; she might make 'em herself," said Mrs. Henry Wycoff. "But they 're just a little bit alike, Mis' Thorn and Katy, and I guess they like to be together. You see my sister-in-law ain't a bit sociable, like I be. When Jared 's gone she stays right to home, to keep things straight, she says; and when he 's there, no mortal could coax her to go visitin', not if 't was to Queen Victŏry's. She sets such store by that poor feller!"

"Katy 's a good wife and Jared 'preciates her," said Mother Wycoff warmly. "In that respect you 'll not find much resemblance atween her and Emily Thorn. And that makes me think of another queer trick of Mis' Thorn's. She 's gone to school every blessed winter since

35

she's married—two winters now—just like the young ones! Jared says she could read and write pretty well when she first come; but now she's fur ahead of any other scholar in the district. She's studyin' some high-school books now, like Jared studied at that big 'cademy in York State."

"John Thorn's got a decent common edication hisself," said Mrs. Spiller, "an' I guess he didn't want his wife to be *too* ign'ant. Now, my man says it's enough for a woman if she can sign a deed or morgitch without havin' to make her mark."

"I reckon John don't hev much to say about Emily's goin' to school or lettin' it alone," said Mrs. Aaron Waldo. "I've an idee his wantin' her to do a thing would be a pretty strong reason with her for not doin' it. They must be hangin' on from sheer contrairiness. Everybody's been expectin' 'em to part for a year past. It's not 'cordin' to the kestom of the kentry for folks to live as they do."

"Speakin' about Mis' Thorn's plain dresses," said Mrs. Henry Wycoff, "I asked her one day at Katy's why she 'most always wore gray flannel. She said because it didn't drabble at the

bottom like cotton did. You see she always
brings up the cows for the milkin', and then
she takes everlastin' long walks besides; goes
away down to the long crossway, 'n that's
more 'n a mile. I asked her why she did n't
hev her things trimmed up a little, with flounces
or a kitterin' piece round the bottom; 'n she
said she'd taken a hint from a remark Mr.
Truesdale made wunst. He had lived a good
deal in cities, and he said there was no use o'
country folks tryin' to foller the fashions, fur
they could n't ony come near enough to be
redic'lous. If they ony knew it, they would
appear much better, to 'dopt some very simple
dress and stick to it. So she always has her
dresses made with a plain skirt that just shows
her feet, and a long, ruther tight-fittin' sack with
plain coat-sleeves. She has a lot of old-fashioned English dimity that was her mother's, and
out o' that she hems ruffles for her neck. She
give Katy a lot o' them ruffles and some fine
linen han'kerchers with colored borders that'll
wash forever."

"Does n't it beat everythin'," said Mrs. Frost,
"to think of her speakin' in that open way of
Truesdale! You know"—this in a lower tone

to Mrs. Kitzmiller—"they've been seen walkin'
along the road, visitin' away as though they
enjoyed it. And Truesdale goes to Thorn's
oftener than there's any need of to see about a
few head of critters he's got pasturin' on John's
fields. John's 'most always away, now'days;
to be sure the old woman's around, but she's
deafer 'n two posts."

"Most likely," said Mrs. Kitzmiller, with an
honest impulse to defend the absent, "she
spoke openly of this Mr. Truesdale, who, I
believe, is a sort of partner of her husband's,
because she had nothing to conceal. It would
look that way to me."

After this neighborly visitation Olive felt an
unaccountable desire to see and know Mrs.
Thorn. She was so young and had suffered so
much. Her husband took her for the sake of a
little money, and there was nothing but hatred
between them. Her neighbors distrusted her,
very probably without reason. And then she
was so beautiful; they all agreed about that —
no one was ever prettier! They had spoken of
her taking long walks, and that awoke a fellow
feeling in Olive; for it was her chief delight,
when her household tasks were finished, to roam

far and free, looking for some pretty place or thing, or, as the mood urged her, for the roughest, wildest nook in all the region. What if she should some day meet Mrs. Thorn! For once a wish came true.

It was on a sultry afternoon in May. There had been showers the night before, and Olive went out to look for mushrooms, where the branches of the beech trees grew broad and low. She found none, and returned to the road just as Emily Thorn emerged from the woods on the opposite side. Their eyes met, and Olive's fell with the embarrassment which is natural upon meeting suddenly one about whom we have been thinking much.

"You are the daughter of our new neighbor, I believe," said the tall woman in the gray dress. Olive nodded bashfully, and the other continued, —

"I would offer to shake hands, but I have been grubbing for these roots for Aunt Thirsa;" and she showed her hand, much soiled with black earth, and holding a bunch of Indian turnips by the tops.

"I was looking for mushrooms," said Olive, but I did not find any."

"Ah, I thought they were truffles. I like them, too, but Aunt Thirsa, who keeps house for us, will not allow them to be cooked."

"Why have you never called to see us?" asked Olive impulsively.

"I might have called," said Emily, "but I do not make calls or visits. We have a queer sort of home — Aunt Thirsa being so very deaf — and people do not seem to care about coming to us. I only go to Squire Wycoff's; they are all the friends I have."

She said this with the manner of one who must go to the extreme of allowable frankness, inasmuch as there was still a world of reserve in her life, which must not be broken in upon.

"I wish I might be your friend," said Olive. Emily turned upon her a look of grave wonder, which softened into tenderness.

"You may, dear child," she said; "there is no reason why you should not be. I will call upon your mother and you to-morrow."

Olive had not thought to look for the beauty of which she had heard so much, but now Emily stopped in her walk and took off her rye-straw hat to fan herself. The slanting sun-rays came through the trees and touched her light-brown hair, turning it to rippled gold. Olive noted the rich effect. She noted also the pure, rose-white complexion, the glowing lips, and the dark hazel eyes beneath brows and lashes almost black. Her face was bright and animated, but as yet she had not smiled. Olive wondered how sweet a thing her smile might be!

The call was made; a very short one, for Emily brought no knitting or patch-work, and Mrs. Kitzmiller failed to interest her in the sowing of late peas and the difficulty of rearing young turkeys when the season was inclined to wetness. Emily seemed very much in earnest when she begged that Olive might come to see her soon.

"To-morrow or the next day, please," she urged, with the wonderful smile for which Olive had been watching.

"She is as good as the best of us," declared Mrs. Kitzmiller to her husband that evening. "I'll venture she's had a good mother, whatever the old man might 'a' been. I found out she was baptized in infancy, and when I offered her a catechism, one of the small ones in purple covers, she said she'd like it as a present from

me, but she knew that book by heart before she
was twelve years old. Just think of that! And
her face is as innocent as a baby's. She seems
lonesome, poor thing, and has taken wonder-
fully to our Ollie."

This was the beginning of long weeks of
almost constant companionship between Olive
and Emily. From the first they treated each
other with the affectionate freedom of enthusi-
astic girl friends. Olive never manifested the
slightest interest about the strange married life
of the other. Between them Mr. Thorn was
tacitly ignored. When they chanced to be
thrown in his company — which was not often,
for he seldom entered his own house, except for
meals — both labored under the same constraint,
and were equally glad to get free from him and
it. His manner toward them was superior and
rather ironical. He sometimes addressed Olive
as Miss Kitz, or made some playful remark to
Emily, of which she took slight notice. It was
not uncommon, however, for him to openly
avoid meeting them; or to look at and past
them, out of cold, dark eyes that had in them
no sign of kindly recognition. Emily had noticed that strange look only since his illness.

In the spring, shortly before the Kitzmillers came, Thorn had had a sharp attack of pneumonia. He had gone to Fort Wayne to make sale of a quantity of leather, and returned home very ill. He went up to his room, bed-chamber and office combined, on the second floor of the currier's shop, and sent Davy Ransom for a doctor. He lay there for three weeks, suffering much, and attended upon at odd intervals by Mrs. Bayless and Aunt Thirsa. From the first he had felt a yearning desire to have Emily come and wait upon him with a wife's thoughtful care. In his utter prostration of strength and will he thought he could gladly die if she would first come close to his side, smile upon him, and touch him with her hands. Through long, feverish days he lay with eyes fixed upon the door, expecting her to enter. Surely some humane, womanly impulse would lead her to visit him, he thought; and when night came, bringing only disappointment, the groans that rent the lonely darkness came more surely from the wounded heart of the man than from the agonized chest in which it labored. Perhaps it was unreasonable that he should expect her, not having given her in any way to understand that her presence was desired, but sickness and love are both proverbially unreasonable. As it was, she never went near him; and he arose from his illness and resumed the usual ways of life with a germ of bitterness in his heart against her.

CHAPTER VI.

DURING the early summer Emily and Olive were almost constantly out of doors. One of their favorite haunts was the long causeway that ran through the jack-oak swamp. It was a corduroy or pole bridge, upon which earth had been thrown till it formed a high, hard road. A narrow ditch ran along either side, in which the water rippled pleasantly, till it emptied into the big ditch, which cut the swamp at right angles with the bridge, about midway of the latter. It was indeed a mighty ditch, such as have been made at public expense in many parts of this marshy country. Its black sides, eight feet apart at the top, sloped down, a distance of five feet, to within fifty inches of each other at the bottom; and the current of water that coursed through it would have turned a mill had there been sufficient fall. Here, where the ditch made its wide sluice under the causeway, was a favorite resting-place for Olive and her new friend. An old jack-oak grew there, with one horizontal branch for a seat, and another in perfect position

for a back to that seat. The two lithe girls
would cross the little ditch with a bound, and
swing themselves up to this rustic perch, out of
reach of snakes, and within reach of the wild
birds' songs, and every richly scented breeze
that blew, and chat and sing for hours. Mrs.
Kitzmiller was always promising Olive the ague,
but she would reply that some people did not
take the ague, and she was sure she would not.
Strange to say she did not.

One afternoon they had taken a long walk,
and were sauntering slowly down the causeway
in the homeward direction. There had been
heavy rains, and a torrent was pouring through
the great ditch, leaving flecks of white foam on
its inky sides.

"How low and level all this region seems,"
said Emily, "yet we are at the very summit
of the country ; right among the water-sources.
I could sail a ship in this ditch, on a voyage
to the Atlantic; for, you know, this water
has its outlet through the Elkhart and St.
Joseph rivers, into Lake Michigan. And I
could sail another on Half Moon Lake, only
a mile south, which would find its way
through small streams into the Wabash, and

on through the Ohio and Mississippi, to the great Gulf."

"Who told you that?" asked Olive. "Did Mr. Wycoff?"

"No," said Emily; "why might I not have learned it in my geography?"

"Because the big ditch is n't down on the map," said Olive, laughing.

"Neither it is, and somebody did tell me, one beautiful day, just about a year ago. He has told me many other things, for he is much wiser than even Jared Wycoff. Poor Jared knows only what he has learned in books, but Mr. Truesdale seems to have been everywhere, and to have seen everything: If we wait here, we will see him, for there is his horse's track. He has gone north since the shower this morning, and will be returning presently."

"Let us go home at once," said Olive; "I do not want to see anyone."

"We will stop and let him pass us," said Emily, "for he is coming now."

Looking northward, through the vista of black-oaks, pussy-willows, and wild-rose bushes, they saw a man approaching on a large red horse. He was with them almost immediately.

Olive glanced up and received a smiling salutation, as Emily introduced them, in a quaint little fashion of her own.

"And this is Sandy," said Emily, caressing the great horse's Roman nose. "Isn't he a beauty? Mr. Truesdale let me name him, so I called him Sandy, because it's Scotch, and just suits his color."

Olive let her glance ascend from the high-topped riding-boot, almost on a range with her head, over a slight, strong frame, to a brown, clear-cut, handsome face, whose dark eyes rested on Emily with a look of such intense and tender admiration that even simple little Olive could not misunderstand it. He lingered a few moments, while Emily fastened a handful of plumy ferns in Sandy's headstall with nice care; then he bowed to both and rode on.

Truesdale's acquaintance with Emily began soon after her marriage. He met her first at Squire Wycoff's, where she stayed a good deal that first year. Wycoff framed deeds and other papers in connection with Truesdale's land sales, and his cabin was his only office. Truesdale had frequent business with John Thorn, and between the two places he met Emily frequently. She was very silent with him at first; this piqued his interest. He exerted himself to entertain her, to impress on her the fact of his personality. By slow steps he drew her on to speak of herself; of her home in Scotland; of the school she had attended there in childhood; of the kirk where her mother took the children every Sunday, and the kirk-yard with its mossy stone wall, inside which two baby sisters slept. She told him all she could remember of the sea voyage, and of the few weeks she had spent in Brooklyn with some Scottish acquaintance of her parents; but when it came to their settlement in the wild woods, and the dreadful years that followed, she was silent.

In return for her small disclosures, he spoke of his own past history; and the glimpses thus revealed made her know that there was another and broader world than she had ever looked into. Her acquaintance with this man was part of the education that had made of her, in the space of two years, a vastly different person from the phenomenally unsophisticated girl that married John Thorn. Truesdale's conversation, even more than Jared Wycoff's books, had changed her.

Davy Ransom had given Emily, that day in the bark-mill, the correct explanation of Horace Truesdale's presence in New Madrid. He had come to Indiana to sell off his land; that business had progressed beyond his first expectation. He had traded and sold, until but little of the swampy tracts of his original ownership remained on his hands. In his extensive rides over the country he had spied out other and more desirable lots, and purchased them on speculation. During his residence in the west he had sloughed off whatever of conventionality he had brought with him. He wore colored flannel shirts and a slouch hat; and his boots, if of a trifle better leather, were thick-soled and high-topped as those of the veriest Hoosier of them all. He was an epitome of contradictions, physical and moral. He had a slight frame, surmounted by a large head, and a face indicative of nervous force, but not of physical endurance. Yet his small, brown hand had a grip of steel, and he could stand his share of exposure and hardship with the toughest of the drovers and trappers with whom he came in contact. He was at home with rough men in rough places; yet nothing like coarseness, or even commonness, ever tarnished his speech or manners. His high breeding was as much a part of him as the distinct, mellow tones of his voice, or the keen, half humorous, yet sympathetic glance of his eye.

He had no need to acquire a liking for wild woods and wild ways. In youth he had been "a roving lad, who thought his home a cage." He had been properly restrained, sent through college and graduated in medicine; but he had never practised his profession a day, and did not intend to. He loved books, good poetry especially; but he loved a gun as well. He loved also, of course, horses and dogs and tamed animals. He loved women in a broadly comprehensive manner. At the age of twenty-one he engaged himself to a girl whom he had known from childhood. Anna Grant seemed to him as perfect a specimen of the bewitching sex to which she belonged as he would ever be likely to find. He was in no haste to marry; but he was careful of his proprieties and gave his *fiancée* no grave cause of complaint as months and years slipped past. He was therefore blankly surprised and deeply sorry when Miss Grant broke the engagement, saying she felt sure he had never really loved her, and she doubted gravely whether it was in his nature to love any woman with sufficient exclusiveness to make him a contented husband. He was disappointed; for some day he had intended to marry, and Anna suited him. Now he was all unsettled again, and it was a question whether he would ever marry at all. There was a good deal in life without that — money-making, hunting, seeing life, studying individuals, human and other.

CHAPTER VII.

AFTER he came to New Madrid, his studies in the line of the "other" afforded him endless amusement, and the other inmates of the Hotel Rounce infinite annoyance. Nothing but Truesdale's gift of popularity — that nameless something which made people always invest him with a Joseph's robe of favoritism — saved him from being ejected bodily along with his happy family. His hounds were always sprawling in the passages, or upsetting swill-pails in the kitchen. Penelope, the tallest one, thought nothing of walking through the dining-room when the table was set, and lifting from the plate a biscuit or slice of bread. He had a tame owl and a crow that were very friendly at times, and again would quarrel frightfully, uttering shrill cries of rage, and making the feathers fly like two furies.

But the most incorrigible pest of all was a pet raccoon. Sam Slick was his master's favorite, but a favorite with no one else. He was a large animal of his kind, fully two feet in length, exclusive of his bushy ringed tail. He was imitative and playful as a monkey, and seemed to be, in the language of the street, always laying for somebody. If a traveller stopped off at Rounce's for a day's shooting, he had to watch well his game bag; for it was Sam's especial delight to insert himself into such a receptacle and mutilate the contents. He was very fond of lying in baskets, and always watched his sly chance, when the clothes were brought in from the drying-lines, to deposit his dusty bulk upon the top of the snowy sheets and tablecloths.

On one occasion a colored boy and another "help" spent a long hot forenoon picking a mess of delicate greens for the hotel table. Truesdale and others of the boarders saw the boys when they returned with a large basketful, and were greatly rejoiced thereat. At dinner, however, no greens appeared, and, when inquiry was made, Prince, the colored boy, explained: —

" Dat tarnal 'coon done spiled 'em. We sot de basket in de londry, till we 'd rested and cooled off a spell, and when we went to look 'em over, dere lay dat bloody critter on top o' dem cowslops we 'd been all de mornin' pickin' !

I shied de clothes-pounder at him, and he jumped about fo' rod."

A murmur of wrath against Sam Slick went around the table, and again he was threatened with death in many forms.

At length Landlord Rounce ventured to say to Truesdale that if he did not remove his pets out of the hotel he would not be answerable for their or his own safety. This led to the hiring of a house for the dogs and the menagerie. It was a little frame box near the hotel, owned by a tailor named Hodges. He had originally intended using it for a shop, but had never gone further at fitting it up than to place a long table under its best window, and decorate its walls with some obsolete fashion-plates and cutters' charts. Hodges liked his wife, and liked her help in his tailoring; she preferred sitting at home with her sewing, so Hodges usually sat there with her.

Truesdale found the "shop" a great convenience in the way of unloading his crowded bedroom of old clothes, guns, fishing-tackle, and the like. He sometimes used the tailor's bench as a writing-table. There was plenty of room on it for his books and papers, as well as for

the gilt wire cage of his little dormouse, and
the larger wooden one of his tame red squirrels.
When he was absent from the village, his pets
were looked after by Susie Hodges, the tailor's
hoyden daughter. In return for this, Truesdale
began to leave his game at Hodges', instead of
taking it to the hotel; and in return for this
again he was frequently invited to take supper
in the tailor's kitchen. There was the usual
amount of winking and coarse joking among the
village neighbors when this growing friendliness
was observed; and before long the assertion
was current that Sue Hodges was "gone" after
Truesdale, but that was all the good it would do
her. He would go back "in yonder" when he
wanted to take a wife. Sue heard of it, no
doubt, but she cared for the pets none the less
faithfully.

If she was seen coming home from the woods
where she had been digging ginseng or picking
berries, with Mr. Truesdale walking beside her,
carrying her basket, she was gossipped about,
but not scandalized. In this primitive community, like most other American ones, the
European idea was reversed; and while a married woman must "walk neat" or bear blame, a

girl under the ostensible oversight of her parents, might do strange things — almost anything, and no damaging word be said. Until wrong-doing became an assured fact, she had the full benefit of charitable doubt.

People grew used to seeing them much together. It was a common thing for Truesdale to ride up to Hodges' door in the early morning with his rifle across his saddle-bow and his dogs behind him; Susie, watching for him, would come out with a basin of parched corn, fill the pocket of his blouse on one side, then go around and fill the other, while he merrily told her where he expected to ride, and what game she might expect him to bring back in the evening.

"Good-bye, black-eyed Susan," he would say, waving his whip-hand as he rode off. And "Good-bye" she would answer back, sometimes saucily, and again with a dreamy cadence, following him with a look of passionate devotion in her dark face.

If Emily changed in the two years immediately succeeding her father's death, John Thorn did also; and he was not improved. No man ever accused him of injustice or meanness, but many accused him of arrogance and harsh-

ness. About his home he was taciturn to
moroseness, and in the world abroad he pursued
his personal ends in business and politics in a
straightforward manner, but often with culpable
indifference to the convenience and interests of
others.

The winter preceding the coming of the Kitzmillers into the neighborhood, Thorn spent in
Indianapolis as a member of the State Senate.
He owed his nomination in no small degree to
Truesdale's efforts in the convention. Even
his best friends declared that a man who cared
so little to conciliate public favor would fail at
the election; but he did not; for in the can-
vass he manifested marvellous ability in handling
his resources, and he carried the senatorial district handsomely in the end.

When he returned from the Capitol in the
spring, Emily met him with more kindness than
she had shown since entering his house. He
noticed it with a rush of keen emotions; but he
had schooled himself well, and considered it ex-
pedient not to recognize at once these relenting
symptoms, if such they deserved to be called.
One day, soon after his return, she asked a favor
of him, and his pleasure in granting it was great;

but in his effort not to let it appear, he chilled her back into her old, torpid, calm aversion. She had long wanted a saddle-horse of her own, and one of his selection, for that would insure its excellence. When she spoke to him about it, he made her scarcely three words of reply; nevertheless, within a week, he called her out to admire a beautiful animal, equipped with costly and elegant trappings. He assisted her to the saddle and let her ride away, never offering to accompany her. The horse's gait was perfect, and he was gentleness itself; so, in a short time, Emily, though unused to the exercise, rode with ease and pleasure. For a while she used her new horse a good deal; but after she became acquainted with Olive Kitzmiller she seemed to care no more for him, nor, indeed, for anything but her new friend. She still went occasionally to Squire Wycofl's, but the coming of a baby into their small house seemed to leave less room for her there than formerly.

In September a startling incident occurred.

CHAPTER VIII.

ONE afternoon, the first time in weeks, Emily ordered Davy to saddle her horse. She mounted him and took a long ride. She was returning leisurely in the evening, and when within a mile of home some one—a woman's form—sprang up suddenly at the roadside and darted across, waving a paw-paw or other large-leaved bush over her head. The horse reared and shied, throwing Emily violently, then galloped home. Thorn was the first to see him, standing riderless at the gate. With a wild horror at his heart he leaped into the saddle and retraced his tracks. He found Emily sitting by the tree against which she had been thrown, bruised, suffering, and bewildered. He knelt beside her, and, for the first time, took her in his arms.

"Poor girl—poor Emily!" he almost sobbed. "Your arm is broken! How will I get you home?"

But Davy Ransom had followed on foot and soon came up panting. By John's orders he

rode the horse back to the farm, and soon returned with a light spring wagon. Emily was
lifted in, half fainting, on a bed of robes and
pillows, and carefully driven home. When
they came to the turning of the road, Emily
roused herself and said, —

"Take me to Mrs. Kitzmiller's."

"Please let me take you home!" John pleaded.
"Why won't you go home with me?"

"I shall die there, alone with Thirsa."

"You shall not be left alone with her; you
shall have a nurse."

"But I want Olive and her mother. I want
nobody else."

"Olive will come and stay with you," Thorn
urged gently; "O yes, you will surely let us
take you home!"

She closed her eyes weakly and resisted no
more. The stuffy little spare room of Thorn's
house was thrown open to the fresh air, and a
bed made there for Emily. Davy was well on
his way for a doctor, and Thorn went for Mrs.
Kitzmiller and Olive. After the broken arm
was set, the doctor left quieting powders to be
given her, under the influence of which she
slept much for several days.

Olive remained with her continually until she was able to sit up in the arm-chair. Thorn looked in often, but did not remain long. Again the hope of winning Emily into a true, wifely relationship was rousing his pulse-beats to a jubilant measure; but he had resolved upon a course of action from which he was determined no outward pressure, no inward impulse, should make him swerve. He would extend to her just so much of kindly attention as she seemed to welcome, and wait for some definite intimation — it need be very slight! — when he might begin to woo her in lover's fashion. He would never startle her again; never let her suppose for a moment that he had forgotten the pledge under which he had induced her to take his name. He often smiled bitterly to himself over that precious piece of folly. If she had taken shelter with the Wycoff's, or lived alone in her hut in the forest, he might have won her as other men win wives. He believed he could have done it; now there was a wall between them of his own rearing, which he must not be the first to pull down.

Entering the room suddenly one morning, Olive saw John standing by the bedside looking at Emily asleep. He turned quickly and went out, but she had caught the expression of his face. Once before she had seen that look upon it. On a certain warm Sunday in July she had arisen from a long nap with a great desire in her heart for Emily, whom she had not seen for two days. She did not go directly to the house, but followed the course of the brook till she came to the tannery buildings. There were no men about there on Sunday, and Olive lingered, eying everything with a sort of aimless curiosity. Passing around the end of the bark-shed, she suddenly came upon her friend, who, engaged with a book, did not perceive her approach. The bark-shed cast a large cool shadow eastward over a bed of dry tan, on which Emily reclined in the attitude of Correggio's *Magdalene* intently reading. Olive made ready to surprise her, when she was arrested by seeing Mr. Thorn approach from the opposite direction. The tan-cushioned earth gave forth no sound, and Emily read on, unconscious of his nearness. Olive was partly concealed by a projection of the piled-up bark, and not wishing to attract notice remained perfectly still. When John saw his wife he stopped suddenly and drew back a pace, as if he felt himself an intruder. Then he stood still and looked at her. Olive will never forget that look. If Truesdale's eyes had expressed passionate admiration, Thorn's spoke a longing agony of grief and tenderness that no language could equal. His firm mouth softened and trembled, and, raising his hand to his brow as if blinded by some mighty weight of feeling, he moved noiselessly away.

Dainty, loving little Olive laid these things up in her heart. Some day she would see her way clear to use the knowledge she had gained with her friend, so charmingly free with her, yet so icily reserved upon this one phase of her life.

A week passed after Emily's injury and she was able to walk about the room and carry her bandaged arm in a supporter without hurting it. Olive went home one afternoon for an hour or two, and in her absence a strange visitor came to Thorn's house. It was the half-breed medicine woman, known throughout the country as Old Bloodroot. She brought a present of wild artichokes to Aunt Thirsa, and through them effected an entrance to the kitchen; then pressed on unbidden to the room where Emily sat alone. She was a horrible looking creature, bareheaded, ragged, and filthy. An enormous goitre twisted her head awry, and her black hair hung in elf-locks about her swarthy face. She stood before Emily and fixed upon her a piercing and sinister look. The poor, frightened girl could hardly find her voice to say, —

" Who are you, and why do you come here?"

The hag replied in a dialect simply impossible to reproduce with letters, but her speech translated into plain English was something like this : —

" You know me well enough, and I come here to tell you that John Thorn is a liar. He has been saying that I frightened your horse. It is a lie! I was sick in my hut that day. Most likely it was one of his girls who hates you ; he has plenty of girls. He hates you, too ; everybody knows that. He would be glad to have you killed. He asked me for my black drops one day — they leave no sign — but he loves his money like a fool, and would not pay enough. He is a beast, a fiend, a son of the "—

Emily sprang to her feet with a wild cry and turned to flee the room, but her strength failed and she sank back fainting into her chair.

When she gradually recovered consciousness she was alone.

From the window of his room in the tan-house Thorn saw the squaw striding across his fields and guessed she had been to his house for some evil purpose. Years before when he bought his land, he had found her squatted upon a corner of it. He let her remain unmolested till she had been caught stealing from his smoke-house and hen-roost, and milking his cows in the woods; then she was summarily driven off the place. Ever after he was the object of her vindictive hatred. It would have been well if, when he hurried into the house, he had related to Emily this bit of Bloodroot's personal history, but he did not. He merely swore roundly at the old witch for daring to intrude her filthy presence, and at Thirsa for letting her inside the house.

"What did she say she came for?" he asked, turning to Emily. In his anger he seemed to demand an answer.

"I don't know," Emily replied, still pale and trembling. "She made me ill. I tried not to listen to her."

All that night Emily lay nervously awake.

The words of the half-breed repeated themselves over and over in her mind, notwithstanding she did not believe them in all their horrible significance. She knew Bloodroot was a bad creature, but people said she was a sort of obi-woman and knew strange secrets. What if John did hate her like that! All the latent superstition of her nature was aroused, and in her weak state, with her imagination unsettled by the free use of opium, the impression made upon her by her weird visitor's words was fearfully strong.

The next morning she anticipated Olive's coming by walking down to Mr. Kitzmiller's. The distance was small, but she reached the house exhausted, and went to bed with a nervous chill. If John was hurt or offended by this rash movement he did not say so of course. He waited two days, then went to see her. His call was a very short one; when he went away Olive followed him to the gate and said, —

"I did not persuade her to come here, Mr. Thorn. We love to have her with us, but we did not know she was coming till she came. That Indian woman frightened her so! Please do not blame me, Mr. Thorn."

His sombre eyes softened into a sad smile as he replied, —

"Why should I blame you for being kind to that strange, lonely girl! I can do nothing for her. She is suspicious, vindictive — I sometimes think utterly heartless. She had better remain here till she gets strong. I shall be away when she goes home."

CHAPTER IX.

ONE day in the late autumn, Davy Ransom was hauling bark from a place in the woods some four miles distant from the tannery. He came home earlier than he was expected, with his team reeking, and himself in a state of strong excitement.

He found Mrs. Bayless in her back yard lifting her stocking-yarn out of the blue-dye pot, and hanging it to air over the horizontal pole that usually supported the soap-kettle. The skeins were tied tightly at short intervals, like chains of Bologna sausage. When, after long soaking and repeated airings, the coloring was finished, the "links" would be a very dark blue, while the tied places would remain almost white; thus producing a clouded or spotted appearance in the knitting. Mrs. Bayless excelled in the production of these choice effects in color. At the moment when Davy came around the corner of the cabin, she was examining a bunch of cross-banded lambs'-wool yarn that Mrs. Henry Wycoff had begged her to put in with hers, the indigo being found.

"Where's 'Zekel?" asked Davy, in a low tone, pregnant with meaning.

"In the shop, I s'pose," was the brief answer. She did not look up, so the boy's air of mysterious importance was lost upon her. He waited a little, then said, —

"I got something to tell him."

"You generally got something to tell most anybody that'll listen to your clack," said his foster-mother.

Davy started for the shop. Mrs. Bayless straightened herself and looked after him, a sudden curiosity dawning in her eyes. He found Bayless in the shop, "slicking" a tanned hide, and opened out at once.

"Say, 'Zeke, I got something to tell ye."

"Tell ahead," said the tanner.

"There's goin' to be a war."

"Where?"

"Right here; and now — to-morrer. I see the forerunners of him to-day."

"The forerunners of who?"

"Why, the enemy! They've pitched ther tents in the five-mile woods."

"Now, look here, Dave; if you don't tell, right off quick, just what you *did* see, I'll take you over this curryin'-board, and make sole-leather out o' ye!"

Davy, not out of terror of Bayless' threat, but because he was quite ready to continue of his own accord, went on to say,—

"I did n't see nothin', on'y a lot of soljir fellers, with ile-cloth caps on. They come with hosses and big kivered wagons. I had n't my load quite all on, but when I see 'em comin', I just climbed up, took the home track, and laid the gad onto Jinny. I did n't 'low to be took pris'ner that a way. I don't go a durned cent on war, any way."

"Did you see any guns or artillery—weepins of any kind?"

"Now, I tell you what, 'Zeke, I was n't skeered so all-fired bad but what I wanted to see more 'n I hed. So when I got most out to the main road, I stopped and hitched Bill to a saplin'; I took Jinny offen the wagon, looped up her tugs, jumped onto her, and rode back to where I could see 'em plain. There they wus, singin' and laughin', hangin' camp-kittles, and puttin' up tents. But I swow the on'y

thing I saw that looked like shootin' was a goll-
blasted machine that stood on three legs, as
high as a man, and hed a little concern on top,
not bigger 'n a hoss-pistol, that a feller was
takin' sight with."

Bayless threw up his head and uttered a great
laugh.

"Why, Davy, you poor little mashed gos-
lin'! Ther ain't goin' to be no war at all!
Them's the surveyors, what's strikin' the line
for the new railroad!"

A day or two after Davy Ransom had re-
treated in good order at the approach of the
"enemy," a young man dressed in a suit of
light gray, much stained with black mud, and
wearing an oil-cloth cap, approached Mr. Kitzmiller's house. He was riding a black horse,
and leading another; both animals were blank-
eted, for it was snowing rapidly.

It was about four o'clock in the afternoon,
and Mrs. Kitzmiller had just emerged from her
kitchen door, and started for the barn to do the
feeding, all her men-folks being absent from
home. She had on a man's hat, and a pair of
boots, and a blue swallow-tailed coat with
brass buttons over her brown flannel dress.

The stranger stopped and dismounted at the large gate of the barn-yard. As the farmer's wife approached, carrying a basket of shelled corn for geese and chickens, he showed no inclination to smile at her grotesque appearance, whatever he may have felt, but lifting his cap, briefly told his business. He wanted stabling for his horses during the storm, and was willing to pay well for it. Mrs. Kitzmiller told him there were two empty stalls, and he might put his animals in, at least for the night.

"There may be right smart of snow," she said, eyeing a bank of purple clouds in the northwest; "but it won't lay; this is only squaw winter; we'll have Indian summer yet."

"I hope so," said the young man. "I belong to the surveying company encamped now on Slater's Run. This weather is hard on our horses, and we find it difficult to get stabling among the farmers, their barns are all so small."

"Yes," said Mrs. Kitzmiller, "I believe ours is the largest around here except John Thorn's, and his is always full with his own beasts and Truesdale's. Here's the fork, sir, and the hay is in the mow. Take all you want for your horses, and while you are about it just throw down enough for my cows and sheep. I'll tell you when to quit. I just came out to do the chores, for my husband and son are both away, and I don't like to climb a ladder if I can help it."

The young engineer scaled the ladder and threw down the hay; then descended and distributed it in long, low racks for the sheep, and in small piles on the lee side of a huge straw-stack for the cows. He insisted upon finishing up the feeding; so, under Mrs. Kitzmiller's direction, he tumbled a bundle of stalks over the fence to a small drove of yearlings in the road, and carried a great basketful of corn to the fattening pigs. Then she urged him to come into the house and get warm. He complied, though he was not cold, and he needed the remaining daylight for his walk back to camp.

They entered by the kitchen door; she disappeared into a back room for a few moments, then returned divested of her masculine garments, as straight and well-favored a matron of fifty as one would wish to see. A model farmer's wife Frank Rossington thought her, in her brown flannel dress, gingham apron, and white bobinet cap. She had a large, bright coffee-pot in her hand, and as she raked out a shovelful of coals and settled it upon them, she remarked, —

"Considerin' how you 've helped me I 'll just make you a good cup of coffee while you dry your boots. Ollie and I took our dinner about the middle of the afternoon. You see we happen to be quite alone ; Leander, my son, went to mill this morning, and the goin' 's so bad it 'll be away on in the night 'fore he gets home. Mr. Kitzmiller 's been gone a week, attendin' Presbytery at Croftonsville."

"Is your husband a minister?" queried the young stranger.

"No, sir, but he was a rulin' elder in yonder where we came from, and he is very anxious to get a supply. There 's no church of our persuasion in this vicinity, and he went to Croftonsville, intendin' to labor with the Presbytery and prevail with 'em, if possible, to send us an occasional supply. We miss the privileges we 've been used to."

"Is there no religious worship at all within

reach of you?" asked Rossington. "I am from the east, and feel a warm interest in these western settlers and everything that concerns their welfare."

"Well, yes," assented the farmer's wife; "the Methodists are pretty strong around here. The Wycoffs are all Methodists, and they are forehanded folks and a strong support to that church. They have preaching and class meeting at New Madrid every Sunday, and at our school-house once in two weeks."

"It seems to me," said the engineer, "that in a community like this one ministry is about all that could be well sustained. I mean, if you could all join one church and work together in that, it might be better at present than to attempt to plant new ones."

"No, my dear sir," said Mrs. Kitzmiller, earnestly. "It is our duty always to contend for the truth; and I know, if you do not, that there is a wide difference between Arminianism and correct Bible doctrine. Not but what I consider the Methodists Christians and their worship better than no means of grace at all. We go to meeting right along, but it don't seem like home to us when we've been used to an

educated ministry. I do hope father will get
the promise of a supply.'

Just then the door opened and Olive rushed
in, cloaked and hooded in brown and scarlet,
shaking the snow from her like a bright beautiful bird.

"I was afraid you would do the work at the
barn, mother, so I brought Davy along."

What a ringing, musical voice! And how
lovely she was — her brown curls all damp and
rough and her cheeks and lips glowing!

"The chores are all done, Ollie; this gentleman"—

"Rossington is my name," he said promptly.

"And Kitzmiller is ours." Thus a sort of
introduction was completed.

For a moment or two the young man and
girl looked into each other's faces. Unconsciously to himself the sudden, deep delight
which he felt in this vision of youth and inno-
cence and girlish charm shone in his warm, blue
eyes. Olive felt it to the quick of her being.
She was dazzled, but not ashamed. When her
own lids drooped it was to hide her timid joy
at being so tenderly admired.

As Rossington was finishing his cup of excel-

lent coffee there was a rap at the door, and
Olive opened it to admit Truesdale.   He had
ridden past the mill that day while Leander was
waiting for his grist, and the latter had asked
him to stop on his way home and tell his mother
that it would be too late when his grinding was
done to start for home, and that she need not
look for him till the next forenoon.

"Much obliged to you, Mr. Truesdale," said
Mrs. Kitzmiller.   "Sit down and drink a cup
of hot coffee.   It's better coffee, I'll be bound,
than you get at Rounce's tavern."

Truesdale had visited the surveyor's camp
and knew Rossington as one of the company.
He wanted to talk with him about the railroad, about anything, for the sake of talking
with one belonging originally to the same world
as himself.   How well and easily their conversation ran on!   Olive listened, wondering and
pleased.

Suddenly there was a tremendous stamping
on the porch and Olive rushed to the door,
crying—

"That's father—I know that's father!"

The farmer entered, followed by a middle-
aged man in black clothes whom he introduced

as the Rev. Mr. Lewis. Rossington supposed at once he was the "supply." Mr. Kitzmiller presently went on to state that the minister had been sent by the Presbytery to look the field over and report. He was pastor of a church at L., fifty miles south, and was on his way home from the Presbytery, making the journey, of course, on horseback. Thus it came about that there met that evening, under farmer Kitzmiller's roof, three men of eastern birth and college training, but of spirits differing as essentially as the lines of their forms and faces.

CHAPTER X.

THE building of the first railroad marks an epoch in any country. It effects a change as potent in its way as the cutting down of the forests, and the letting in of sunlight to the soil of its hills and valleys. During the winter following the survey the business and social life of New Madrid and vicinity received a telling impetus. Hundreds of men found employment in cutting timber and clearing out the swamps along the line, so that everything might be in readiness for the construction of the road-bed early in the spring. Property took a sudden rise. The last of Truesdale's swamp lots went off rapidly; and Leander Kitzmiller paid for the school-section he had purchased on a year's time with the money he received from the sale of half of it. Portable mills and shingle-cutters planted themselves along the streams and water-courses, and the hum of the circular saw was heard in the land. The village, which was the county seat, promised itself a new court-house the coming summer. Several new dry-goods and grocery firms sprang up, their proprietors being, for the most part, young and single men. They, with two lawyers and a new physician, all bachelors, paired off conveniently with the same number of attractive village girls, Susie Hodges among the number. There were a great many sleigh-rides and dancing parties that winter. Truesdale never joined in any of them; though free and friendly with everybody, he had never mingled in a general way in the social life of the place. He attended church, however, and one Sunday night stepped in ahead of young Walters, of the grocery firm of Walters and Gay, and escorted Miss Hodges home.

"I want to talk to you, black-eyed Susan," he said, when they were out alone under the stars; "I want to talk to you about your dreadful flirting. It's not the way I've trained you to do. I don't like all these strange fellows dangling after you. I don't like all this sleigh-riding and dancing."

"Do you really care?" she asked, lifting her face in the moonlight — her face which said as plainly as words could say, — "If I have made you care, it is all I have aimed to do."

" You have been as kind as ever to Punch and
Judy " (the red squirrels) "and to Tiny Tim,
and Penelope ; and Sam Slick tells me you even
made a fire in the den that coldest night while
I was away, but you are changed to me."

She lifted her face again, and saw the mocking light in his eyes.

"You don't care no more for me than that
dead tree over yonder," she said, in a low, quiet
tone.   "I know who you do care for ; it's Em
Ludlow."

The words were out, and she was frightened
at herself for saying them ; but her companion
went on smoothly, —

" I care a good deal for Mrs. Thorn, partly
because she is such a lady. She never says
'don't care no more,' or 'have saw,' or 'had
went.'"

" I suppose you have taught her better," said
Sue bitterly. "I wonder who sent you out
here for a missionary to train all the wild girls
in Indiana how to dress and talk."

Truesdale laughed a low, merry laugh of
genuine amusement.

"That was splendid, Susie ! Mrs. Thorn
never said anything I liked as well. She is not

at all given to humor, and she never gets so delightfully angry as you do."

They had reached Hodges' gate. She snatched her hand from his arm, and exclaimed hotly, —

"I suppose I am not a lady, and never can be!" Tears of smothered passion and wounded pride stood in her eyes.

"You are a sweet, bright, warm-hearted girl," said Truesdale, encircling her with his arm and drawing her gently, but firmly, to him. "I am sorry if I've hurt you. I do not care to have you much different. I like to see you run and leap across little brooks and walk squirrel-bridges. All your movements are so strong and graceful. And I like to hear you sing and laugh, and even whistle; but those barbarisms in speech! — and you could so easily drop them."

"I will," she whispered; "I know better, and I will try. And I won't go with Mr. Walters again if you'd rather I wouldn't."

"As you please about that," he said with a smile. "I was only teasing you;" and dropping a kiss as light as a lingering breath on her cheek he left her.

He knew well she would not please. She indulged in no more gay parties and rides, but pored secretly over her grammar until she had mastered its intricacies and stumbled no more in her verbs. Love was the despot who forced her fickle, girlish memory to do its work like a drudge.

During the winter John Thorn was more than usually occupied with business, and was a good deal away from home. When there, he seemed studiously to avoid meeting Emily. The irregular ways of the household made this comparatively easy of accomplishment; frequently there were days together when Emily caught but casual glimpses of him. For a long time she had instinctively shunned his presence, not that she feared him or found him personally disagreeable, but from a sense of constraint growing out of their anomalous relationship. Still it hurt her as nothing else had ever done to know that he regularly planned his movements to avoid crossing her path. At times a sense of loneliness swept over her, deeper and more absolute than anything she had suffered alone in that forest hut with her decrepit father. Of the possibility of a happy understanding with John she never dreamed. He had made no positive move in that direction since that day at the gate, a few weeks after their marriage. She did not desire him to approach her in that way again, and she did not think he ever would. She still believed his chief purpose in marrying her was to secure her father's money; perhaps there was less of it than he had expected, and he was bitterly disappointed. He had the air of a disappointed man.

Emily and Olive saw rather less of each other than when they first became acquainted. This was in part owing to the fact that Olive was attending Jared Wycoff's school, and Emily had concluded not to go. She was steadily acquiring a deeper quietude of manner. She had been seeing more of people this last year, and they pressed too close. Her life was not just like the lives of others, and she must keep to herself. She did not mean to be reserved with Olive, and Truesdale would not let her be stiff and silent with him. Almost unconsciously to herself she had come to regard him as her chief source of entertainment. He visited her openly, though not with conspicuous frequency, and she scarcely thought of what the outside world would say. She was trying to forget there was an outside world.

Her Sundays were usually spent at Mr. Kitz-miller's. She would dress early and ride with them to church in the village. Upon their return they would have dinner, and after that an hour's Bible study around the sitting-room fire, with Drs. Scott and Jacobus in helpful readiness near the farmer's elbow. Then the two girls would escape to Olive's room, where — strange indulgence for that time and place — they were allowed a cosey fire in a little square cast-iron stove about the size of a raisin box. It was on such a Sunday afternoon that Olive showed Emily her valentine. She had carried it in her bosom for two days and slept with it under her pillow. In appearance it was only a letter in a white envelope. It had so happened that she had taken it from the post herself, and the secret was wholly her own.

OLIVE, — I heard your pretty name only once, and I saw your pretty self only once, but I have forgotten neither. I think I can never forget any little thing connected with that stormy November evening. I was just thinking how cosey the kitchen seemed, and how bright and genial your mother was, when you entered, and I saw nothing, thought of nothing else, while I remained. Forgive me if my eyes spoke too plainly what my heart felt. I thought you turned away quickly, as though offended by my look. I had no time to guard myself. How good you seemed !

"I was afraid you would do the work at the barn, so I brought Davy along!"

Such a liquid, loving voice! And the sweet, impulsive running to meet 'father' and helping him off with his snowy great-coat. How good, indeed, but more than all, how bewitchingly beautiful! I fell rapturously in love, and shall remain so till I die. I expect to see you — well, before many months have passed, and I shall read in your eyes whether or no you are displeased with your presumptuous   VALENTINE.

"It is a delicious love-letter, Olive," whispered Emily.

"That is just what I should call it," said Olive, laughing softly, while her eyes grew bright and the warm color rose to her temples.

"How strange," she said, "that I should have been thinking of him every day — a great many times every day — and then, that he should write me this letter. It has made me very happy, but now I am going to burn it. I intended to do so all the time, because I could not show it to mother, and it would be wrong to keep it a great while without. I wanted you to see it, so that afterwards, when it seemed like a dream, I could ask you, 'did I ever get such a letter,' and you could tell me 'yes.'"

CHAPTER XI.

ON a certain soft evening in April, Olive sat
by the sitting-room window, busily crimp-
ing and plaiting her mother's cap-borders.
Mrs. Kitzmiller was putting the finishing touches
to her evening's work, and the farmer himself sat
just outside the window, on the verandah, reading his weekly paper. The air was full of that
peculiarly western melody, the low, continuous
chirp of frogs, and the tinkle of cow-bells could
be heard when one thought to listen. It was so
warm that the door stood open, framing a picture
of lambs at play in the near field, with a back-
ground of hazy sky and budding forest. It was
suddenly darkened, and Olive, glancing up, saw
standing there the civil engineer in apparently
the same mud-spotted suit of gray, with his cap
in his hand, and his blue eyes pouring their warm
light upon her. Dame Kitzmiller had seen him
and came forward with extended hand.

"I've been wonderin' lately, Mr. Rossington,
if we shouldn't see you back here this summer."

"It was a piece of good luck, Mrs. Kitzmiller," he said; "they don't often employ the surveyors to work up the grade, but I very much wanted to come, and managed to get on the force."

Mr. Kitzmiller came in and welcomed the stranger as if he were a tried friend. It was the way of these simple, kindly people; they knew no other. Olive scarcely looked up. After the first wild rush of color to her face, the blood receded, leaving her pallid and cold. Rossington waited for her to offer her hand, as is the free custom of the West, but she did not do it; it trembled so. Her face had a white, constrained look which it pained him to see; he took it for displeasure. Nevertheless, he followed out his original intention in coming that evening.

After talking awhile with the farmer and his wife about matters connected with the new railroad, he told them he was one of a corps of six engineers who had established their headquarters at New Madrid. Just then he was engaged in making the estimates for that part of the road which ran near Mr. Kitzmiller's land, and he would like to engage board for a week or two at the farm-house. He had not forgotten how generously they had furnished stabling for his horses that stormy time last November. No objection was urged against his staying, and Mrs. Kitzmiller, on learning that he had had no supper, went out to prepare that meal for him. But he followed her into the kitchen, and, seating himself at one end of the carefully scoured table, implored her so earnestly for a bowl of bread and milk that she at length set it before him, insisting, however, upon supplementing it with a plate of thick maple-sugar cookies and some delicious crab-apple preserves.

While Frank Rossington leisurely enjoyed these delicacies, he inquired of Mrs. Kitzmiller concerning church matters, and learned that as yet they had only secured an occasional "supply." A Mr. Sweden came from Romney, distant twenty-five miles, when he was not prevented by ague or bad roads, and preached in the court-house at New Madrid on Sunday morning, and in the school-house in their neighborhood in the evening. He had good congregations, but as yet no attempt had been made to organize a church.

"I suppose," said the young man, "that his

work here is regarded by the Presbytery as
missionary labor."

"Well, not exactly," replied Mrs. Kitzmiller.
"Mr. Sweden is pastor of a pretty strong
church at Romney, and he said if he could receive one hundred dollars from this place, he
would come here once a month, for a year.
Dan'l guaranteed that sum. He said to me
that he guessed we'd better make it up our-
selves the first year, and not appeal to the
people; I said maybe we had, though I couldn't
see how we'd do it, without selling something
we couldn't really spare. But John Thorn
questioned Leander about the matter, and one
day, not long ago, he stepped in and handed
Dan'l twenty-five dollars, as his payment
towards Mr. Sweden's support. He never
goes near preaching himself, but lately she's
taken to goin' with us quite reg'lar."

"I think, Mrs. Kitzmiller," said Rossington,
"that we engineers will be able to help you out
in the matter of your minister's salary. We
shall be around here perhaps a year, and we
have all been used to an educated ministry."

The next morning, Frank went from the
breakfast-table, which was always set in the

ample kitchen, into the sitting-room, and found
Olive there alone. Mrs. Kitzmiller detained
her worthy husband to say to him that, now
that this stranger was with them, he had better
not read a whole chapter at morning worship,
and, above all things, not to be lengthy in
prayer. One ought to guard against making
religion tiresome to the young, and she knew
Mr. Rossington was in a hurry to get off.
Kitzmiller quoted the adage that "prayer and
provender hinder no man's journey;" but she
continued, as though she did not hear him, that
often, in the busy season, she had herself
thought she could have prayed twice while he
was praying once.

"Indeed, mother," said the farmer, mildly.
"I think if you always prayed *once*, while we
are on our knees, the time would n't seem so
long."

While this little colloquy was going on in
the kitchen, Frank was trying to establish a
friendly understanding with Olive. Over night
he had arrived at the conclusion that the valentine was a stupid blunder. She would, of
course, consider such a declaration as it contained, coming from a stranger, as highly pre-

sumptuous, unless she had been as deeply
smitten as himself, which was not at all likely.
As for himself, he was entirely satisfied with
his own condition of mind. He had always
expected to tumble into love headlong; he considered it the best and surest way. And this
darling girl! He would win her yet; but first
of all he must make his peace with her. This
he tried to do, standing near her with his lofty
head bent a little, that he might watch the look
of her half-averted face.

"I might better have sent you one of those
cut-paper arrangements, with gilt doves, and
hearts with arrows through them," he said.

"Yes, they are beautiful," laughed Olive.
"I have one or two that I got when I was
little."

"At any rate, I did not mean to vex you,"
he said. Then she told him she would not be
vexed any more, and he thanked her earnestly.

She could hardly keep the tears back till she
was alone. Her letter, that had tinted life with
the rosy hues of sunrise, had been only a boy-
ish prank; something for which — now that
they had accidentally met again — he ought to
apologize. Her tender heart was very sore.

What a strange misunderstanding! Her embarrassment had seemed to him displeasure, and his efforts at conciliation had led her to think him a gay trifler.

If either of these young creatures had surely known, a fortnight before, that they would soon be domiciled under the same roof, what secret raptures each would have indulged in! But the time thus spent was not at all rapturous. Rossington was away from early morning till sundown; but he spent all his evenings at the farm-house. Sometimes he smoked a friendly pipe with Mr. Kitzmiller on the verandah, and talked with him and Leander about western politics and the prospects of the country, or explained the mysteries of his profession. Kitzmiller was something of a mathematician, and had a great admiration for what he called "fine head-work." Consequently he was much interested in the methods of calculating curves and gradients. Olive usually had her place near the open window, for the weather was warm as June. She loved to listen to Frank's deep, mellow voice while she watched the fire-flies light their tiny lamps across the misty meadows.

Sometimes they had the talk to themselves. She was not shy with him now, but chatted in a frank, bright way about many things. He began to get acquainted, and found it worth while to learn something of her opinions and tastes, for she really had both. At first he had thought only of her fresh beauty, her engaging manners, and of the affections whose existence he thought were revealed in her face.

CHAPTER XII.

THEY talked one evening about the wild, wooded country, which Olive professed to like after a year's residence in it. Rossington reviled the marshes, and Olive found a good word to say for them.

"You ought to go through the long marsh just north of Loon Lake, in June," she said. "It is like this," drawing an emphatic little line on the window-sill with her finger; "there is a bridge running through the marsh, half a mile long, and on each side the bridge a ditch, of course. Along each ditch is a solid border of blue flag, — wild iris, you know, — which blossoms just when the dog-roses are out, a close hedge of them, four or five feet high, without a break. Growing through and above the rose-brush are all the rich, green things you find in swampy places. Just think of that vista of color! Bright blue, with dashes of yellow near the ground, and, above, a blended, waving mass of pink and green! Have I given you a little bit of a glimpse of it?"

"Yes," he responded, "and a scent of it, too. I am going to see Loon Lake marsh in June. Perhaps you will be kind enough to show me the way."

She made no reply to that, but presently continued, —

"Browning once said to a friend in Belgium, that he liked the quiet Norman country 'because it was not obtrusive, like some more pronounced landscapes, but left him to make its beauty with his adorning fancy.' I think he would have liked northern Indiana."

"How apt!" said Frank admiringly. "I can never remember anything I read, to use it in that way."

Olive smelled daintily at a little clove-apple which she had picked up from among the knickknacks on a table near her. A smile dimpled her cheeks, as she said demurely, —

"I ought, perhaps, to confess that I found that in a newspaper, and committed it carefully to memory, to have it ready for some such occasion."

How mischievous she looked! He had never been so deeply in love as to-night.

"I fancy you read a good deal," he said.

"Where do you find books in this wilderness?"

"Squire Wycoff has a good many that I can have the use of; and Mrs. Thorn has purchased quite a library, under his direction."

He went away the next day, and did not return for a week. One Sunday afternoon he rode out from New Madrid. Emily was with Olive; they were reading in the parlor, which was always open on that day, and did not see Rossington till he came up the verandah steps. He was daintily fresh in his best "go-to-meeting" clothes, and his hair had been newly clipped, leaving it in close, brown waves. Olive looked at it; he noticed the look, and laughingly asked her how she liked his summer contour. She did not answer very promptly.

"I was thinking" — She stopped and turned to Emily, who seemed to guess her thought, for she broke into a little laugh, in which Olive joined, with a bright blush.

"I believe I know what you were not going to say," said Emily.

"Why not say it?" queried Frank.

"I *will* say it now," said Olive; "it would be ill manners not to, after all this hinting. I just happened to think of something we read last week, that a great Frenchwoman — I can't pronounce her name — once said. It was that a woman should count herself fortunate who had seen three handsome men in her life."

"I am curious to know who the other two might be," said Rossington, with easy self-assurance.

" Mr. Thorn and Mr. Truesdale," replied Olive promptly.

"Yes," said the young man, in a reflective tone, "Thorn is a magnificent fellow, with a strong, true face, and carries himself just as a man of his size should. Truesdale is small, but symmetrical, with a Roman profile, and an aristocratic head and hand. I will leave you to complete a description of number three, while I go and talk with Mr. Kitzmiller;" and his tall, slight figure moved gracefully out of the room.

"I 'm afraid I seemed very bold," Olive said, a troubled look coming into her face.

"I think not, dear," replied Emily. "I thought you seemed very winsome."

"I am not myself at all when he is here. I was silly about that valentine, and I have been so afraid of his guessing it ! "

"Poor Olive!" said her friend; "do not think of it or him. The world would be a better place if there were no men in it."

Rossington found the farmer and his wife in the wide, clean kitchen, where they both felt most at home. Mrs. Kitzmiller was dozing over the church-paper, and her husband sat with "Boston's Fourfold State" shut lightly on his brown forefinger, while he smilingly watched the gambols of a pair of half-grown kittens. He glanced up with some surprise as Frank stepped into his range of vision. Ordinary Sunday visitors were disapproved of; but there was nothing ordinary about Rossington, and it taxed one hard to disapprove of him in any capacity.

Mr. Kitzmiller got up to bring in the broad, splint-bottomed chair from the porch, — the one he had expressed a liking for. Frank took it, and chatted an hour with the worthy couple. When he rose to go he handed Mr. Kitzmiller a folded paper, saying, —

"I have been able to do something among the engineers in behalf of Mr. Sweden's support in New Madrid."

It proved to be a subscription, payable on

demand, amounting to seventy-five dollars.
Rossington's name headed it for a third of
the amount.

He came and went, but seemed to get no
nearer Olive. She was not diffident, but she
was elusive. His admiration was very open,
but very respectful, and she accepted it without
the confusion he would have rejoiced to see.

One bright forenoon in May he stopped at
the farm-house, and found Olive ironing on the
back porch. A low, broad-topped walnut threw
all the place in cool shadow. He took a seat
near her table and watched her work; she
seemed a little pensive, and he scanned her
face narrowly. Presently he made her sit
down and read a long, loving letter he had just
received from his widowed mother. Olive's
heart glowed with pleasure, and a soft color
rose to her cheeks as she read that mother's
expressions of pride and confidence in her
"brave, good son." Then they stood together
at the end of the stoop, and watched a great
white hawk circling slowly against the deep
blue of the sky.

"I am going now down to the deep cut," said
Frank, suddenly. "I will be back towards
evening."

Towards evening Olive went out to bring in her ironing from the rack. There sat Rossington, in the chair he had occupied in the morning, toying with a cigar, and looking as though he might have been there all day. In fact he had come but a few minutes before. Olive gave a surprised exclamation, and the rich blood mounted to her brow. She went directly to the rack, and commenced transferring its snowy burden to her round arm. When she turned to re-enter the kitchen door a passing breeze caught up a fleecy undersleeve, carried it lightly and laid it down at Frank's feet. He captured it quickly and went up to replace it atop of the glossy heap. There was a slight, uncontrollable tremor when he came so near, a little start and flutter; the white mass toppled, slipped, and, spite of her efforts to save it, tumbled down to the floor. Olive uttered a cry of dismay and a nervous laugh.

"It was all my fault," said Frank. "I am very sorry!" and he went down on his knee to assist in gathering up the ruin. The larger articles were easily lifted all together, but many of the lighter ones came unfolded and went fluttering about in the treacherous wind. Frank and Olive invariably reached for the same thing at the same time; the girl grew dizzy with confusion.

"Never mind," she said; "I'll just bundle them all in and refold them on mother's bed."

With reckless haste she crushed together collars, cuffs, and kerchiefs, and was gliding away, when Frank stopped her.

"Olive, wait." The trembling hands threatened a fresh mishap.

"I'll not let them fall again," he said, and encircled her and all she held in his strong, steady arms.

"Olive, I want you for my wife, and I want your answer now. I am aware you know but little about me, but I am not afraid to have you learn; and your heart will tell you — here so close to mine — whether it can ever love me."

She lifted her maiden face, so pure and tender; Rossington kissed it with a murmur of endearment, then let her go. He went straight into the room where the farmer and his wife sat in the gathering twilight, and asked them for their treasure.

CHAPTER XIII.

I HAVE just three little cares," said Olive, in one of her post-betrothal confidences with Emily. "The first is mother. Poor, dear mother! She grieves so over the thought of losing me! I blame myself daily that I do not feel more distress about leaving her; but this new love — ah, I cannot speak of it! It changes everything! Nothing else could make me willing to leave my parents."

"Your mother esteems Mr. Rossington highly," said Emily. "She told me so. She also trusts him entirely, and rejoices in your happiness. I think when Leander brings his wife home, as he probably will before many months, she will not be so very lonely. But I shall be desolate! No one else can take your place with me."

"Yes, that brings me to my second care. You will miss me; but you have missed so much besides. That is the saddest of all. O, Emily, I cannot be selfish enough to accept my great happiness without wishing a like joy to my dearest friend! If you only —"

"Hush," said Emily, in a low tone, turning pale. "Let that alone. Let me alone. What is your third care?"

"Frank's mother. He tells me she will be suited with his choice, and says every kind, re-assuring thing he can think of; but I have not heard from her yet. She cannot separate us, but I should grieve to be a source of disappointment and regret to her."

They were real cares to the gentle girl, but they only weighted a little, as was necessary, a heart too buoyant with love and bliss. Leander suggested another drawback. The thought of it had flitted across her mind, making the shadow of a moth's wing.

"I'll tell you what, Sis, you'll be a badly scared kitten in a strange garret. I wouldn't be caught that far off my own stamping ground for the price of a load of clover-seed."

"Neither would I," said his sister; "but a load of clover-seed don't begin to compare. I shall not be scared. Mrs. Rossington isn't very fashionable, and I can keep still and learn. It will be a matter of dress and little forms, and Frank will help me."

One afternoon Rossington asked Olive, almost as soon as he came, to walk with him down to the old beaver-dam. Back of the house at a field's distance was a little hill; going down the farther slope one came upon a clear brook, the same that ran past Thorn's tannery, farther along. Between the knoll and the stream was what remained of an ancient beaver-dam, and growing upon it were large-trunked yellow and white willows. On the slant hill-side was a scattering grove of young maples, and beneath one of them the lovers seated themselves. The place was bright and breezy, but very secluded, and it suited them well. Frank drew forth a letter and laid it in Olive's lap, saying,—

"It is from mother."

"Oh! what does she say about — me?" Olive whispered in a little flutter of hope and apprehension.

"It is for you, love, look at it; open and read it."

"My Dear Girl, — Frank has sent me your picture. You have a sweet face; and if you as truly love him as he does you, I kiss and bless you for my daughter. I have known his secret a good while, for I am one of the fortunate, though often perplexed, mothers to whom

their children go with unreserved confidence. Do you
know — I suppose he has told you a score of times —
that he fell in love with you the first moment he ever saw
you? I approve of being in love; even of falling in love.
I only urged Frank to go and make your acquaintance
in your own home, amid your familiar surroundings; to
make sure of himself, and then make sure of you. This,
it seems, he has done, and I congratulate him. I also
congratulate you. You have won a noble heart for your
own. So kind and devoted a son and brother cannot fail
to make a tender and faithful husband. My two married
daughters are very curious about you, but, like myself,
they strengthen their wondering souls with the reflection that *Frank's choice must be all right.*

"Please write me a little letter in answer to this, and
believe me,

"Very sincerely and affectionately yours,

"HENRIETTA ROSSINGTON."

Olive sent in reply a prettily worded but
rather stiff little missive, which, however,
seemed to give much pleasure to its recipient,
The married sisters wrote, not to Olive, but to
Frank; and one of them suggested that, when
he brought his bride east in the fall, Olive should
provide herself with nothing but a plain travel-
ing suit, and have her trousseau bought and
made in Albany. Frank laughed merrily at
that.

"You see, dear, they are afraid you will not
be properly gotten up. They want to oversee
the shopping and dressmaking."

"There are good grounds for their fears," said
Olive; "I believe I will take their advice. It
will save mother a lot of worry."

"You are an angel!" Frank cried. "It was
a piece of impertinence in Louise, and any
other girl would have got angry about it."

One evening he brought two of his fellow
engineers out to the farm-house and introduced
them to Olive. Messrs. Bonn and Sayward
had both seen her at church in the village, and
thought she seemed rather ordinary; like many
country girls, she did not appear at her best on
public occasions. That evening, however, they
followed her with eyes only less full of pleased
interest than Rossington's. She wore a dress
of sheer lawn, with cherry ribbons in her hair,
and a babyish coral necklace around her creamy
throat.

An old-fashioned round centre-table stood in
the middle of the little parlor. It held a great
flower-pot; not a spray or two in a bouquet-
holder, but a mass of June roses, red and white,
what you would wish to carry in your arms.

There were some other things on the table, —
a plate of "friendship cards," and some bamboo
ornaments from India, brought, of course, by a
returned missionary. Olive carried everything
away to a stand at the side of the room, except
the flower-pot. Then she went out, and presently returned with four great saucers of straw-
berries on a salver. Her mother followed with
the sugar-bowl and a pitcher of cream. She
acknowledged Rossington's introduction to his
friends with a curtsey to each; then said, turning to Frank, —

"If you'd only said a word, I might have
made some queen's-cake, or some other kind
that's good to eat fresh with berries."

"That's all right, Mrs. Kitzmiller," said the
young man; "but if we just had some maple-
sugar cookies now" —

"You know we always have those," said the
cheery dame, and bustled out to bring a plate-
ful, while, at Olive's bidding, the three gentle-
men drew up to the little feast spread forth on
the round table. She poured the rich cream
over their fruit, then took her own saucer, and
ate her berries daintily. After this the other
engineers called with Rossington at different

times to see his "wildwood flower," as he loved
to call her."

Ah, that glorious June, rose-crowned and
daisy-shod! Those two ardent young souls
held up the goblet of life together, while the
radiant goddess poured it brimming full of joy.
To them the growing freshness and brightness
of the dawn brought the thrilling promise of
love's old yet ever new delights. Each morn
was filled with the large, glad hope to which all
things are possible; and the purple haze of the
slow twilight was no softer than the mellow
content of their loving, fearless hearts. But if
Holbein or Dürer had pictured them, it would
have been with a pitiless Fate following in their
shadow, mocking them with satirical laughter,
and pointing with skeleton finger to an unseen
peril in their path.

CHAPTER XIV.

IT was in the last week of July that the shock of an awful calamity fell upon the little company of civil engineers in New Madrid. A gloom which was the gloom of death extended throughout the village, the Wycoff settlement, and to many other settlements, near and remote.

One brilliant morning Rossington went down the road on a hand-car, over a wooden tramway which had been laid for some miles out from New Madrid, for the convenience of engineers and laborers. Mr. Bonn was with him. When they reached the point where the road touched a corner of the Kitzmiller farm, Rossington stopped the car. He had an armful of wild marsh blossoms, mallows, golden-rod, monarda, and vervain, with spikes of vivid lobelia flowers.

"Wait here just five minutes," said Frank, leaping down the embankment; "I want to carry these up to that house."

One of the navvies who propelled the car

stepped down and seated himself on its side, and deliberately took out his pipe.

"Mr. Roshington's sure to make his five minutes twanty, so we might as well enjoy a bit of a shmoke. I've waited for him here afore."

His companion followed his example, and young Bonn amused himself by throwing pebbles at a gray squirrel, that scolded him noisily from the top of a tall sapling. Frank cleared the space between the road and the house with long, swift strides; he approached from the rear, and Olive went out on the back porch to meet him. She took his flowers and laid them on the bench, merely saying, —

"I'll rave over their beauty when I make up the flower-pot; now I have n't time."

All she seemed to have time for was to stand folded in his warm embrace, under the shadow of the low walnut. The men-folks were afield, Mrs. Kitzmiller in the spring-house; they were quite alone in the balmy summer stillness. Olive stood on the low step of the porch, and her lover on the ground; so she was just high enough to press her soft cheek to his, again and again — a favorite caress with her. What need to repeat their words — the unfinished sentences, the tender nothings that mean so much?

"I must go," he said, at length. "I'll have to-morrow afternoon to myself. Get all your work done, dear, and wear the tea-rose lawn and the red beads."

"Shall I walk with you down to the orchard fence?" asked Olive.

"No," he replied; "we'd be in sight of the road there, and you wouldn't let me kiss you. We'll say good-by right here."

She loosed her clinging arms, and said, with her hands resting lightly on his shoulders, and her eyes drinking in the tender light of his, —

"Tell me something, Frank, — the sweetest thing you know, — to think of till to-morrow."

"My darling oh, I love you!" he whispered, with kisses between the words; then released her, and went with fleet steps back to the car.

About noon a low rumble of thunder was heard in the west; it continued, scarcely increasing in loudness, till two o'clock, when a dense black cloud began to appear above the forest line that belted the horizon.

"I wish Emily would come over," said Mrs. Kitzmiller; "she's so afraid when it storms, and she's all alone with Thirsa."

Olive was standing in the door, looking towards Thorn's.

"Would you care, mother, if I went to stay with her?" she said. "She doesn't come here quite as often as she used. Maybe I've seemed to neglect her, though I haven't meant to. Hadn't I better go at once?"

"Yes, Ollie, run right along quick, and get in before the rain comes. There comes father and Le to the house; I'm glad they started in time."

Olive ran off, and in five minutes she was with Emily, who had gone up to her bedroom in a great horror of loneliness and dread.

"Come down and watch the storm gather," said Olive. "It is the very best way to get calmness."

She drew her friend down stairs and out of the house. They stopped within a few seconds' run of the door, and together stood and faced the angry west. Wreaths of thin white vapor floated hither and thither over its greenish darkness, and the forked lightnings shot in every direction. Emily turned and looked at the young girl's radiant and unflinching face.

"It seems to me like the wrath of God," she said.

"It is grand and awful," said Olive, " but it does not seem like that to me. I have known only the love and goodness of God all my life. If I were to be stricken to death here and now, it would not — it could not — be by a wrathful blow. God is my Father, whom I love and trust."

Just then a flock of crows, which had been routed from their high-built nests in the tamarac swamp three miles away, came flying on the wings of the wind and adding their doleful cawing to the terrific elementary confusion. The two girls ran in, for the great drops were falling.

"Frank will get a drenching, I suppose; he is out in that direction somewhere," Olive said.

Emily at once looked alarmed.

"The wind," she said, " has been much worse out yonder, and there is timber everywhere."

"Yes, but there are cleared fields and farm-houses within reach; they would see the storm coming and seek shelter. Mr. Bonn is with Frank, and I fancy he would do some lively running to avoid a wetting." She laughed lightly as she thought of the young man's rather foppish care of his person.

The storm lasted two hours; the thunder was continuous and loud, but not startlingly near, and the wind was high and steady. It did not come with the hurricane's rush, but its force was very great; the broad, low house jarred in its clutches, and the crash of falling trees sounded through the dash and pour of the rain like the boom of minute guns. It was over at last, and Olive went home. The world looked as if a miniature deluge had visited it. There were gaps in the forest, far and near, through which the blue sky shone. These openings, making the landscape strange, marked the spots where trees had fallen, generally the largest of their kind, weakened by age and decay. Scores of these century-crowned forest kings had yielded to the blast,—among them the hollow tulip tree which old Ludlow had chosen for his treasure chest.

Olive found her mother with a look of deep anxiety on her face.

"What time would the hand-car go back?" she asked.

"As soon as possible after the rain stopped, I should think," Olive replied. "It may have passed before now."

"No," said Mrs. Kitzmiller, "I have been watching the road." Still the happy girl had no fears for her lover.

Late that evening Mr. Truesdale rode up to the house. Both himself and his horse were covered with mud, and the animal was panting. Something in his appearance alarmed Mr. Kitzmiller and his son, and both went out to the road as soon as he halted. There was a low-spoken sentence or two, then Leander said hoarsely, —

"Great Heaven! Who will tell her? It will be her death-blow!"

Rossington and Bonn had taken refuge in a farm-house, as Olive had said, till the violence of the storm was over. Then they started back to the road where their car stood, intending to return at once to New Madrid. They had some rods of thick timber to traverse, and, when midway, Frank was stricken to the earth by the sudden falling of a great branch which the storm had loosened. Bonn's cries brought to his assistance some laborers who had sought shelter in the side of an embankment. Together they carried Rossington back to the house he had just left, and a messenger was despatched to the village.

Then in what wild haste they rushed out there to that lonely cabin in the wilderness! The engineers, the doctors, friends who had learned to love the genial youth, strangers who had only seen his handsome face — over the slippery, miry road, under cracking and falling boughs, they galloped with reckless speed! Truesdale and the surgeon, upon whom John Thorn had pressed the use of his fleet, strong horse, were soonest there; but the life they had risked their own to stay was ebbing fast. The crushed skull was raised; everything was done that could be done, but all to no avail. When Truesdale came to Kitzmiller's it was to tell the worst, and to say that they were bringing him there to the house of his friends.

Two days later there was a brief and touching funeral service, in the presence of an assembled multitude, who had left their harvest labors far and near, drawn together in self-forgetful sympathy over this appallingly sudden death. A quartette of the engineers broke the solemn hush with an appealing hymn.

> " Peace, be still!
>   In this night of sorrow bow,
>   O my heart, contend not thou!
>   What befalls thee is God's will —
>   Peace, be still!

> " Lord, my God!
>   Give me grace that I may be
>   Thy true child, and silently
>   Own Thy sceptre and Thy rod —
>   Lord, my God!"

None who that day heard the music of those rich male voices, surcharged with deepest feeling as they were, can ever forget its heartbreaking sweetness.

His five associates followed as mourners when the body of poor Frank Rossington was borne to its grave in the shadow of the maples, near the old beaver-dam, with its growth of fluttering aspens and waving willows. It was supposed to be only a temporary resting-place; for when the railroad was finished his mother would doubtless desire his removal to the family plot, near his eastern home.

Pale, pitiful little Olive was strangely quiet through it all. On the first morning after the death she said to Mrs. Kitzmiller, who was almost distracted with grief and horror, —

"Do n't cry so, mother, or you will make me cry. I must keep from that while he is still here with me."

She did not forget his request, but when the afternoon came she dressed herself in the tea-rose lawn, and put on her pretty necklace.

"O, how can you dress like that to-day?" said Emily Thorn. And Olive replied, —

"Frank said, yesterday morning, he would be with me all this afternoon, and told me what to wear."

Then she went in, and sat for hours, gazing upon the dear, still face, quite natural and un-injured, till every line was imprinted upon her deepest memory.

"You have met with a great sorrow," said Mr. Sweden, when he came.

"Yes," she responded earnestly, "a sorrow great enough to fill all my life, no matter how long it may be!" There was a pathos in the tone and words that caused the minister's heart to swell till further speaking was impossible.

She however continued, in the same strange voice, like that of one who bled inwardly and was calm in the face of death, —

"But not great enough to cloud my trust in the wisdom and goodness of God."

"May He bless and comfort you for those words."

She looked up with her dry, mournful eyes, to see the strong man's face drenched with tears and convulsed.

With what fearful suddenness that wild storm came and passed! When all was over and quiet, the great bouquet of marsh flowers still bloomed brightly in the blue jug on the table. The wild bees soared in at the open window, buzzed about it for a moment, then out and away, hovering next over the fresh earth of that new grave on the hillside.

CHAPTER XV.

PEOPLE who watched Olive Kitzmiller in the days succeeding Rossington's death wondered immeasurably at her calmness. Some even concluded the blow had not hurt her deeply. Others, who knew better, apprehended a sudden breaking down of health or mind along with that marvellous self-control. They need not have feared. The soul within that dimpled, girlish body was upborne by more than mortal strength. She suffered! The black wine of bereavement gave out for her all its pungent bitterness. A thousand stings of disappointed longing pierced her tender bosom daily. Yet she was not without consolation. No language could express the sense of rich possession she enjoyed in the memory of that precious love! It would never weaken or grow less. His last words to her, "*My darling — oh, I love you!*" must forever repeat themselves in her thoughts, bringing, in the dim years to come, a thrill of grateful joy more heavenly sweet than the living companionship of husband

122

and children! She helped her mother, waited upon her father, and took long walks as usual with Emily Thorn. No one saw her weep. The tears were quick to fill her soft brown eyes, but she never let them fall. At night she relieved her heart with crying; she could never have slept else.

She longed, yet dreaded, to hear from Frank's mother. At length a letter came; its penetrating sympathy was hard to bear. The elder woman felt no jealousy in her great sorrow, but recognized the younger woman's right to mourn even for her own idol.

"O, you poor child!" she wrote. "How will you bear it? You are so young, and youth is so unreasoning in its grief! For me it is but another tie loosed. I have resigned much; I can resign him when I have agonized a while. In a very little time these sharp struggles will be over forever with me, and I shall rest with my beloved; till then I must keep my heart in patience. But you have not had the schooling in losses that time brings to all, and this must be very bitter! I wish I could see you. Some day you must come and stay with me, but just now we might not do each other any good.

Tend well my dear boy's grave. If he sleeps in a pretty place, and it would pain you to have his body removed, it need not be done."

Friends and neighbors came to Kitzmiller's, drawn thither by the mingled sentiment of curiosity and real sympathy; but when they saw Olive they could not speak of her trouble. On one occasion old Mrs. Wycoff was spending an afternoon with her mother. Olive was sitting alone on the porch with some sewing in her hands, and heard them within talking of Frank in a low tone. She caught the words,

"If he had only left a clearer evidence!"

Something prompted her to rise and go in; something prompted her to say,—

"You were talking of Frank as though he might be a lost soul. How can you, mother, who knew him, imagine such a thing?"

"I do not imagine it, my child. I know he is in the hands of a wise and merciful God; but we dare not mistake amiability for grace."

"If I were to be killed suddenly, would you fear for my eternity?" asked Olive.

"No, dear; you are a baptized member of the visible church, and the child of many prayers."

"So was Frank, if it will comfort you to know it. He was more; he was a confirmed member of the Episcopal Church, and had taken the Holy Communion, which I never have."

"Who taught you to say 'the Holy Communion' in that way?" said Mrs. Kitzmiller. "It is a phrase of Popery."

"See, mother," cried Olive, "this was in his breast-pocket when he died. He always carried it." She drew forth a little book of devotions, and laid it in her mother's lap. Its prayers and lessons of deepest spirituality had been to Olive an unspeakable solace; but the elder woman — tender mother, earnest Christian though she was — looked askance at the cross on its cover, and pushed it aside as though it might be a thing of danger.

The autumn days drew on, and Olive received a letter from Mrs. Rossington, begging an invitation to come at once to Indiana. She longed to see the people who had last seen and talked with her son. She wanted to see his grave before the snow covered it. She would not trouble them long, but would they receive her for a few days? She was not very strong, but she was sure she could bear the journey, perhaps better than in the spring.

Olive showed the letter to her mother, who read it and bent her brows in reflection.

"It is the conceit of a troubled mind," said the farmer. "I wonder if she has thought of the fifty miles of rough staging at this end of the route. If she would wait till spring, the new road would bring her to our door; but she might not live till spring, and an unsatisfied heart is a sore thing to carry. What are you studyin' about, Lucy? You surely can't misdoubt our ability to make the poor lady comfortable for a short spell."

"Dan'l, you vex a body! If I ain't always dilatin' and explainin' my thoughts, you're afraid they're not of the right sort. I was just debatin' whether to let Mrs. Rossington sleep in the parlor bedroom, or give her the spare chamber that's warmed by the sitting-room stovepipe. It'll be cold before she gets here."

"I'll get a new stove for the parlor," said Kitzmiller. "Them stairs is steep and narrow."

One bright October afternoon Olive and Mrs. Thorn were sitting under the trees in Mr. Kitzmiller's yard. They had been talking of Mrs.

Rossington's expected arrival, and of many other things, when, looking toward Emily's home, Olive saw Truesdale dismounting at the gate.

"Do you see Mr. Truesdale very often?" she asked.

"No, not now," was the answer. "He and Mr. Thorn have always a good deal of business together, but I always go away when I think he may be coming. Do you know, Olive, I heard what those women, Mrs. Frost and the others, said about me at your house that day soon after you came here. Katy Wycoff told me not very long ago. Other things have been said at other times and places. I am an unfortunate woman, but I am an honest woman; it could never be possible for me to be anything else. And Mr. Truesdale is the truest gentleman I ever knew."

After a little pause she continued, —

"I hardly dare think what would happen if any one would say such things to John Thorn. I do not deserve to have enemies, but I am afraid I have. Who could that strange woman have been that frightened my horse last autumn? I can see her yet, and it was not old Bloodroot.

If they could make him believe there was anything improper about me, perhaps he would kill
me."

Olive started in horror.

" O Emily ! How can you think of such a
thing ! He could never harm a hair of your
pretty head. *He loves you!* "

It was Emily's turn to start.

"Olive, hush ! How dare you say that ! "

" Because I believe it — I *know* it."

"No," said the other, "it is not true. Because you love me so well you think he must ;
but you do not know him. You have heard
how he married me ; everyone has heard that.
I think he grows more tired of my presence
every day. I am becoming an insupportable
burden to him, and I have a sort of expectation
that before long a crisis will come ; he will find
some pretext for shaking me off. I will await
the issue and do nothing to hasten it. I have
been the victim of circumstances all my life,
and circumstances may do their worst. A
while before you came I would have gone away
from here, if I had known where to go. Since
then, my Olive, I have been almost happy. I
am thankful I have been with you so much ; it

shows the gossipping world that I am fit to be received by such correct, Christian people as your father and mother, and allowed to be intimate with their only daughter."

The next day Mrs. Rossington arrived at the farm-house. Olive had seen her picture; she had prepared herself to meet a woman tall and fair, because Frank was tall and fair. At first she could hardly adjust her ideas of Frank's mother to the small dark lady, whose penetrating eyes searched everything and everyone with such keen yet kindly interest. The tones and accents of her voice in conversation recalled her son to the Kitzmillers; like him she was given to asking questions about matters that were novel and strange to her. She had lived almost all her life in large cities, but she was country-born, and a thread of childish associations familiarized her at once with the homely routine of farmhouse life. She wore plain but rich clothing, and carried an elegant watch in her belt; but she frequently busied her slim hands with Mrs. Kitzmiller's coarse knitting-work, and followed the farmer's wife into kitchen and spring-house, honestly delighted with the nice order everywhere observable, and honestly entertained by the unpretentious yet shrewdly intelligent conversation of her hostess.

She made her first visit to her son's grave alone; after that, she and Olive sometimes went together. Sitting there one dreamy afternoon by that newly sodded mound, upon which the maples were sifting a slow shower of gold, she told Olive of a second reason for her visit. She had come to confirm her judgment in the wisdom of a design she had in mind. It was to make over to Olive the share in Frank's estate which in law had reverted to her, his mother, as his nearest heir.

"I do not need it; his sisters do not; neither do you, just now, but I think it would please him. It pleases me to do this for his sake, and because I love you."

"I thank you," said Olive, "most of all for the love." After a little silence, she said softly, slipping her hand into that of the elder woman, "It may help me to live well the life I have marked out. It will be a lonely life, but it need not be an altogether unfruitful one."

"Frank used to write me of your sweet, strong voice, — I have never heard you sing, — and he intended to have you educated in music after marriage. Do you ever think of that now?"

"I think of it," Olive replied, "as something to do in the future. But just now, this year, I can do nothing, go nowhere. I must stay right here with my aching sorrow till"— The sentence was finished with falling tears.

A little later a smile came into her pale face as she said,

"I shall never forget Frank's amusement when I said to him one day that I knew there was not a piano within a range of four counties, and that Emily Thorn had never seen one in her life."

"Your friend Mrs. Thorn interests me very much," said Mrs. Rossington. "I should like to see her husband."

"She interests every one," said Olive, in response to the first remark; and then she asked, "Has she ever spoken to you of her husband?"

"Yes, once," said the widow, briefly.

CHAPTER XVI.

FROM the first moment of their first meeting, which occurred the day following Mrs. Rossington's arrival at Kitzmiller's, Emily Thorn had felt strongly drawn toward the strange lady. There was an air of quiet strength about her which distinguished her from every one with whom Emily had associated. A succession of varied and deep experiences had left their impress upon her, disciplining judgment and will, and making her one whose estimate of the conditions and possibilities of life must, in the nature of things, have more than common weight. She was a wise woman; Emily felt this, and when she found she was accessible, she hardly cared whether she was sympathetic.

They had an hour to themselves one day, and Mrs. Thorn suffered this new friend, from a thousand miles distance, to look into her domestic life far enough to be able to understand that it was one of strange complications and precarious continuity. At the close of the interview Mrs. Rossington said,

"Where would you go if the day should come when some inexorable cause would constrain you to leave this place?"

"I do not know," said Emily. "I am a stranger in the land."

"To have no tie of blood in the wide continent — I can imagine the sense of isolation it must give. But if that day should come, and I am alive, let mine be the friend's house to give you welcome."

"You are boundlessly good," said Emily, her smile bright with tears.

That day came, — sooner perhaps than either anticipated. Mrs. Rossington had been gone but a short time, when the crisis arrived of which Emily had spoken to Olive shortly before her coming.

It was the evening of a perfect Indian-summer day. Emily had been enjoying it out of doors, and was sitting by the west window of the bare little sitting-room of her house, watching the hazy sunset, and resting after her walk. Thorn entered suddenly; she made a little startled movement, but did not rise. After waiting a few moments, that she might not seem abrupt, she rose quietly and was about to leave the room, when he addressed her in a voice of suppressed passion, —

" Mrs. Thorn, I wish you would stop here, and give me your attention for half an hour. I think I never made so large a demand upon you before."

She turned and looked at him, then resumed her seat by the window, with a face as pallid as the dead. John stood by a table, nearly in front of her; his breath was hurried, as if he had been walking rapidly, and he drew forth his handkerchief and wiped the thick drops of perspiration from his brow. He took from a long, leathern pocket-book some papers, and while unfolding and arranging them he said, — "I have not the slightest notion, Emily, of what you have been feeling and thinking all these months and years. I only know that to me life has been almost unsupportable. But the grand mistake has been one of my own making, and I could go on as I have done, if I did not think there might be something better, or at least pleasanter, for you."

Then, resting his hand on the table, and assuming unconsciously an attitude of superlative strength and grace, he looked full at her and said, —

"*I am going to give you up to Truesdale.*"

"John Thorn!" she cried hotly, "do you believe me to be a guilty woman?"

"No," he answered promptly, with a strange smile, half bitter, half tender; "you do not look like that. You are not that now, and I do not want you to become so."

He turned to the papers again.

"Here is your property — bank certificates, notes, and securities for the entire amount, except three hundred dollars, which I paid on the Morse land, when I bought it, soon after you came here. That land cost a thousand dollars, and here is the deed; I had it drawn in your name at the time of the purchase, as Wycoff can tell you. And here is fifty dollars of my money to fee Bolton or Lee, or any other lawyer you may choose, who will file your petition and secure you a divorce. Court is in session now, and you may have your freedom inside of ten days if you move in the matter promptly. You can proceed on the ground of incompati-

bility, if you will; or if you feel at any loss
for a cause of action, the court will furnish you
one; they keep a list on hand. The precious
divorce laws of this God-forgotten State were
made for just such cases as ours."

He folded the papers, put the money with
them, and returned all to the pocket-book,
which, after carefully securing the strap, he
handed to Emily. She took it mechanically,
and rose to her feet.

"You may go now," he said.

"But where shall I go?" she asked, her
tender voice breaking in a childlike way.

"Anywhere, away from here," was the cold
reply. "Truesdale will not leave you long in
uncertainty. He will see you soon, but he cannot talk with you under this roof."

Still she hesitated and lingered.

"I saw him not three hours ago. He took
great satisfaction in saying how ardently he
loved you, and how deeply he pitied you."

"You *saw* him!" she demanded, flushing red.

"Yes, I went to his office on business, and
while there I accidentally brushed down from a
shelf a handful of dried weeds. He picked
them up and put them carefully away, saying,

as he did so, that the woman he adored had once trimmed his horse's bridle with those ferns. I understood him, as he intended I should; and in about five minutes he understood me. He stands ready to marry you the moment the bond between us is cancelled. He does not despair of being able to win your love, though there has never been a word or act on your part 'inconsistent with the most disinterested friendship.' You know how the damned jackanapes hunts around for long words."

She walked to the door in a bewildered way, then turned and looked at him again. She felt a sudden strange impulse to throw herself upon his breast and beg him to keep and care for her. But she remembered that he had *talked with Truesdale*, and her cheeks burned again. She took her hat from a bench on the porch and went away in the deepening twilight.

A while later she tapped at Kitzmiller's kitchen door. The farmer himself opened it and exclaimed upon seeing her, —

"Why, it's Mrs. Thorn! Come in, come in! How queer you look with that big, black pocket-book! Have you been robbing somebody?"

"No, I have done nothing," was the reply; "no harm to anybody in the world; but John Thorn has turned me out of doors."

Olive's arms were about her in an instant, and she sank down slowly upon the calico lounge near the door. Then a look of surprise came into her eyes, and a smile, wan enough, but with pleasure in it, flitted over her face.

"I believe I am going to die!" she said, and, with a long sigh, fainted quite away.

Late that night she was able to tell Mrs. Kitzmiller and Olive what John had said before sending her away. When she had finished Mrs. Kitzmiller asked, —

"Are you glad or sorry that this has happened?"

"It had to come," was the reply, "and I would not undo what is done; but I am glad for nothing. I feel injured and humiliated and utterly sad. I am more forlorn than Hagar, for she had her little boy. What a contempt I have always felt for Abraham! Mrs. Kitzmiller, my greatest anxiety now is, that you and Olive may not think ill of me for the strange position in which I am placed."

"Don't trouble yourself on that head," was

the good woman's instant reply. She was standing before Olive's bed on which Emily lay, touching, from time to time, the rich-colored hair and white forehead with the corner of a fine towel wrung out of camphor-water.

"I can see how it came about. It has all grown out of your singular way of living with your husband. It has been a good deal talked about, and Truesdale came to think he had a right to like you. I don't believe you ever knowin'ly gave him that right, but now I suppose you will see him and listen to him."

"I will see him once after what has passed," said Emily, "but I will see him only in your presence, and listen to nothing that you may not hear."

"But you will get your bill and marry Mr. Truesdale, as Thorn expected?"

"I shall sue for a bill as he told me to do; he wants his liberty and he shall have it. Perhaps he wants to marry again — I almost think he does — but I do not. He may cast me off, but he cannot dispose of me. How careful he was to give me back the money!"

"He never cared for that money," said Olive, kneeling by her friend's side. "It is perhaps

too late now, but I ought, weeks and months
ago, to have made you know how earnestly I
believe that he married you for love and love
alone. He did it in a stupid, blundering sort
of way; yet I am sure he loved you."

"Olive, you do not know what you are saying," Emily responded. "It is impossible for
one like you to comprehend a nature as cold
and hard as his. Perhaps he came to wish me
— to be more to him than I was, but I held
him to the letter of the bond; and he grew
weary and chafed under it. I was handed over
to him by my father as an incumbrance with
that bit of money; now he is glad to thrust it
and me away from him."

To this aspect of the case, that she was,
through no fault of her own, a homeless outcast,
she recurred again and again, till towards morning, when she fell into a feverish sleep.

CHAPTER XVII.

DIVORCES were common in northern Indiana, and they were not uncommon in the Wycoff settlement. Jared Wycoff's youngest sister had been twice married and twice divorced, and was awaiting, in her father's house, a third opportunity. The grounds upon which divorces were obtained were as often ludicrous as serious. They ranged all the way from cold feet, and flies in the pudding, to drunken cruelty and the graver cause recognized by Scripture. This door stood plainly open before Emily, but she had never contemplated seeking her liberty through it. She scarcely needed more personal liberty than she enjoyed. She had often longed for escape from a false position, but that she should ever take any steps towards achieving it seemed impossible. Thorn's desire to do so had once or twice made itself apparent to her; but she had always done him gross injustice. Hers was a nature in which impressions took root and grew, false ones as readily as right ones. She believed him

141

to have been actuated in the first place by avarice
alone ; any personal sentiment he might have for
her must be basely secondary.   That he had for
years cherished for her a passion as pure and
chivalrous as that of any red-cross knight never
entered her imagination.

Twice she had been strongly inclined to leave
him ; once soon after his illness, of which we
have spoken, and again after her recovery from
the injury she received when her horse threw
her.   Each time, the reaction he experienced
from hope to despair told on Thorn's face and
manner; and she attributed his avoidance of
his home and of her to dislike and weariness.
Her absolute loneliness stood in the way of her
taking any decisive step.   Even then she never
seriously thought of joining the endless pro-
cession which filed through the divorce courts.
The traditions of an orderly, Bible-reading
ancestry tinctured all her blood.   She came of
conservative and essentially respectable people.
Her poor, half-crazed old father was perhaps
the chief sinner of them all; and he sinned
strictly within safe domestic limits.   In the
home of the Kitzmillers, with their Puritan
beliefs and ways, she found a congenial atmos-

phere. Mrs. Kitzmiller herself could hardly have recoiled more surely from the suggestion of divorce for the sake of other marriage than did Emily, when it was put barely and boldly before her by Thorn. Truesdale had never appeared to her in the light of a lover. His open admiration, his delicate yet persistent attentions, had glanced harmlessly from the armor of innocent ignorance, of modest self-esteem, that encased her. That evening's work, however, changed everything. Creation had lapsed into chaos, and the shocked atoms must be reconstructed into new forms.

Out of the confused whirl of impressions which thronged her mind upon awaking from a few hours' slumber, one or two ideas were distinctly formulated. Her moorings were loosed, and she was adrift on the current of circumstance. A near and certain contingency was a meeting with Horace Truesdale, and all that it implied. He had loved her while she belonged to Thorn — allowed himself to love her, knowing his love meant dishonor to her and treason to the friend he had more than once been pleased to describe as "the finest fellow upon earth." Yet he had loved and pitied her; a

thrill of gratitude pierced her heart. His was
a nature whose generous warmth would sun a
woman's life into bloom and beauty! Her
thoughts flew frightened away from the subject.
but ever came back like drunken insects to
poisoned honey.

As Thorn had said, Truesdale did not long
leave Emily in uncertainty. He called early in
the forenoon at the farm-house and inquired for
Mrs. Thorn. His manner toward Mrs. Kitzmiller was that of grave deference, while he
noticed Olive but slightly. His face was pale
and somewhat anxious, and he looked as though
he had not slept.

Mrs. Kitzmiller persistently refused to be
present at the interview, which was not a long
one. The good woman was much tumbled up
and down in her mind, and went about her
morning's work in an excited manner. In such
moods she talked rapidly, and dropped her final
g's with reckless indifference as to effect.

"The idea of such a state of things bein'
possible!" she said to her husband, who sat
near the kitchen door, scraping a new axe-helve
with a piece of broken glass. "To think of a
strange man talkin' love to a married woman,

right here in my own house, and we a lettin'
him ! But what can a body do ? I can't in my
heart blame that poor girl for any part of this
miserable business, unless it 's for not tryin' to
like her man after she was tied up to him.
She 's just had the queerest luck that ever a
mortal was born to, and I pity her from my
very soul. And Truesdale, seein' how the
plaguey laws were here, just laid out to get her.
And it seems John Thorn was only too glad to
let him have her."

"I don't believe Mr. Thorn is glad at all,"
said Olive. "He was jealous, and angry, and
cruel, but he is not glad to be free of her; he
is perfectly wretched to-day. Emily thinks he
wants to marry some one else, but I feel sure it
is not so."

"Anyhow, he has no business to want to,"
resumed her mother; "nor she either, for the
matter of that. It's a miserable mess, and the
disgraceful divorce laws are to blame for it. If
people did n't know they could get free just for
the askin', the Old Harry would n't put mis-
chief into their heads half as often as he does.
Not that I think he 's ever put any into Emily's;
she 's as good as the best."

So she fumed and worked, stiffening up her bread-sponge, and clear-starching a few fine things of Olive's, which had been put by from the plain ironing. Presently they heard the front door open and close, and a little later they saw Truesdale ride away from the house.

In that interview of an hour Emily's attractiveness with Truesdale was immeasurably enhanced. He found her pallid and listless, anxious only that their conference should close speedily. When he spoke of his desire to make her his wife in the event of her becoming legally free, she blushed, and her heavy eyelids drooped. After this momentary confusion she told him in a steady voice what she had said in substance to Mrs. Kitzmiller the night before. She intended procuring a divorce, more on Thorn's account than her own; but she did not intend to marry. She was grateful for his pity, his interest, his condescension in offering his name and protection to one so homeless and almost friendless. Then his studied self-restraint gave way, and she was forced to listen to the most ardent protestations and pleadings. He censured himself for precipitancy, and bewailed the fact of his having plunged her into a vortex of annoyance and trouble, urging as his only excuse his earnest desire to make her ultimately happy, and his confident belief in his power to do so. She interrupted him with a sudden gesture of appeal, and begged him again to leave her.

He remembered, as he rode away, that the weary indifference of her manner had dissolved and given place to a tinge of warmer life; that when he rose to depart she had lifted to his face tearful eyes full of confidence, and had suffered him to take her hand and kiss it. He remembered also that she had forbidden him to attempt seeing her again while she retained the name of wife.

CHAPTER XVIII.

AT the end of a month the decree of divorce had been granted, and Emily Thorn had gone from the Wycoff settlement. Her destination was known to the Kitzmillers and to one other person, and it was their secret. Immediately after the separation she wrote to Mrs. Rossington and received a prompt reply, renewing the offer made in the conversation recorded a few pages back.

"Come," she wrote, "and share my quiet home, for a time, at least, till some door opens in the blank wall of the future."

After the reception of this letter Emily brightened a good deal. Olive felt hurt at the eager longing she manifested to be gone.

"I am not glad to leave you and your dear mother," Emily said, in reply to a gentle reproach; "I grieve to give you up, but you are all I have to leave, and I can bear it for the sake of putting behind me all the rest. I am not one with this community, and never have been. I have been regarded with suspicion

148

and dislike always; as something foreign and strange, though I have interfered with no one. If I had been ugly I might have been accused of witchcraft, so eccentric have I seemed. Ah, yes, I shall be quite warm and cheery when I am far away! My life has been so bare and cold; only for you, Olive, I should have frozen quite!"

Truesdale begged earnestly for the privilege of accompanying her at least over the earlier and rougher stages of her journey eastward, but she refused.

"If I may not accompany you, I will surely follow you," he said.

"I dare not allow it," Emily answered. "Mrs. Rossington has never taken you into account when extending to me her incomparable friendship."

"I will never compromise you with Mrs. Rossington," said he, "but I am quite determined to be taken into account, first or last."

A little smile, which was half a grimace, flitted over her delicate face as she said, —

"I had fully determined to run away from you with all the other annoyances."

"Do I annoy you?" he asked earnestly. "I

am very sorry. How can it be when I love you! And I believe you love me, or will."

"You feel for me the deepest, kindest sympathy, and always have; and my heart goes out to you in gratitude. O Horace — there, I have called you that to show how I trust and like you — put yourself out of the question for a while! Let me depart alone and in peace! Time will tell whether we need each other as you think. I am tired and do not want to be agitated with any strong emotion for a great while — for ages and ages! I shall have rest where I am going, and the companionship of a wise and good woman; it will be enough."

"It will not be enough," he said, "or I am deceived in you as I have never been in woman before. But you shall have your way and your time. Some day, however, you will see me in Albany. I am going to leave New Madrid for good and all, some time this winter; and what would be more natural than that I should return to my boyhood's home on the Hudson, a few miles from that city? Mrs. Rossington is no stranger to my name and my family, nor, indeed, to me. I wrote her, jointly with Sayward, the letter that gave a detailed account of her son's

last movements, and of his death. Then, too,
I chanced to be at Fort Wayne when she reached
that point on her journey here this fall, and we
made the stage-ride in company."

" So Olive has told me; and that you kindly
made business for yourself at Fort Wayne about
the time of her return, and accompanied her so
far on her homeward journey; but what of all
that?"

" Simply this, that I have had my introduction. Since your latest plans have been made, I
have taken the liberty to write to Mrs. Rossington, telling her plainly of my desire to marry
you, and begging her good offices toward that
consummation. I think I have made it clearly
apparent to her, that any ordinary objection to
divorce and subsequent marriage must be
markedly wide of application in this particular
case. I do not expect an answer, but I am not
afraid of my reception by her, when I call upon
you at her house, some weeks — or years shall
I say? — hence."

Emily's preparations for departure were soon
made. Olive was helping one day with some
sewing. They had worked in silence for an
hour, when Emily said, —

"How strange that *I* should be going to spend the winter in Albany instead of you!"

"You have spoken my very thought," said Olive, with the piteous little smile that always accompanied her strong efforts at self-control. This time her efforts failed. Her regret at parting from Emily, added to her other deeper sorrow, was too much. Her breast heaved with a great sob, and she put by her work to save it from a shower of tears. Emily held her in her arms and smoothed the wavy brown hair, while the poor, loving child wept on her shoulder, till she could weep no more.

"Poor Frank!" were her first words. "I wish I could get over this unutterable pity for him! He was so young, and loved life so well! His happiness is greater in heaven, I suppose, —I believe; but he was happy enough here, and he would have chosen to stay — with me."

She lifted her head quickly, threw aside her tear-wet handkerchief and pressed Emily's fresh one to her hot eyes; then she took up the sewing again.

"Don't work," said Emily, "if you do not feel like it."

"But I do feel like it," she responded; "it is

a pleasure to do things for people, and this needs to be done to-day."

The day before Emily took her departure Squire Wycoff called to conclude a business settlement, he having acted for her as a sort of trustee since her father's death. They were quite alone during this interview. When all was finished Emily expressed her thanks warmly for the thoughtful interest he had always manifested for her welfare. A sudden wave of deep feeling swept into his pale, sensitive face, as he arose and took up his hat and cane.

"It is none of my concern, perhaps," he said, "but I have had a heartache over this break-up."

"You are too kind," said Emily; "pray do not feel for me so deeply. I shall soon be far away where gossip cannot reach me, then it will be easier to forget. The worst is over now."

"Pardon me, my dear friend," said Jared, but it is not for you I feel the most. You will be consoled, but John Thorn never will."

"He thinks he has done right, and will not suffer self-reproach as you suppose."

"You misunderstand me again. He has,

perhaps, less cause for self-reproach than for
self-pity. But I reproach myself. I helped to
set his heart on fire with expectation. When
he spoke to me of his long-cherished love for
you, and his plan for obtaining you, in a sense
against your will, I told him to go on. I told
him an honest, manly, self-conquering passion,
such as his, must, in time, win in return. He
never broached the subject to me after your
marriage day; I knew he was living the life of
a starving man in sight of food, but I never
lost faith in my own prophecy till I heard of
your sudden separation. Yes, I feel for him; I
almost fear for him. Though he is a grand
specimen of physical perfection, and I am what
I am, I would not change places with him this
hour if I could."

He shook the fair, soft hand that had suddenly grown icy cold; repeated his wife's mes-
sages of remembrance and farewell, then said
gently, reluctantly, —

"Well — good-by, good-by."

She stood where he had left her for a minute,
passing one cold hand over the other. From
the kitchen came the cheerful sounds of table-
setting, the burr of the coffee-mill, and Mrs.

Kitzmiller's voice talking with some one who had just come in. She turned and left the still room with its deepening shadows. It was Davy Ransom who had come in; he was sitting by the stove and looked up with his usual good-natured grin when Emily appeared.

"Good-evening, Davy," she said; "so you have come to bid me good-by. I am glad you thought of it."

He made no reply to this, but drew the back of one mittened hand across his eyes. Presently he got up and started off; at the door he paused, and beckoned Emily to come out. She picked up a little shawl from the lounge, threw it over her head and followed him outside.

"I got something to tell ye, an' something to gin ye," he said, backing up against a post of the verandah.

"What have you to tell me?"

"That cute little smooth-handled mallet I made ye to chip bark with, ye mind. I'm goin' to keep that's long's I live to 'member ye by."

"You may keep it, Davy; I like to be remembered."

"And ye mind that fall ye husked corn with

me in the field beyant the sap-bush? Ye said
one day ye wisht ye had a cute little peg that
'ud just fit yer hand. Well, I made ye one,
but ye did n't come to the field no more, and I
never gin it to ye. I brought it 'long to-night.
Maybe ye won't need it where yer goin'; but I
made it for ye anyhow."

She took the husking-peg of polished hickory,
with its finger-strap of soft buckskin, and looked
at it carefully in the dim light.

"It is a very good peg, Davy, and you were
very kind to make it for me. I will keep it
always to remember you by.

Still he lingered.

"I reckon you 're awful mad at yon feller?"
motioning towards the tan-house, at an upper
window of which a light burned. She said
nothing, and he went on, —

"I 'lowed to tell ye, ye could n't be wuss out
with him than he 's out with himself. He just
walks! I wunst saw a caged critter to a show;
he walks like that — nights, I mean."

"How do you know what he does of nights?
You know you are the hardest sleeper! Nothing can wake you."

"I kin wake myself when I 'm a mind to, and

I hev for three nights now, and crep' into the shop at midnight. He was walkin' up there — boots on — had n't had 'em off."

He was silent for a few moments, then broke forth with a great, gasping sob.

"O, Lord! I can't stand it to see him ack so and not do nothin'! He 's done for me ever since my dad and mother both gin out with the fever the same year. I was n't eight year old." He was crying.

"Good-by, Davy," Emily said; "I must not stay here any longer, it is very cold. Go home, now. Good-by."

He dashed his mitten across his eyes again, and said, half defiantly, as he shuffled off in the darkness, —

"A dog may love a man, an' I 'm no wuss 'n a dog."

CHAPTER XIX.

THE change from New Madrid to old Albany was a very great one; but Emily was less bewildered by it than she had anticipated. Her constant and varied reading had familiarized her thoughts with methods of living other than those she was personally accustomed to. She met with few things that were totally strange to her knowledge. Her new home was one of elegance and refinement, but she was not utterly lost in it. She had seen such homes in books, and visited them in her dreams.

Mrs. Rossington lived in close retirement, her daughters and a few chosen friends forming the very small circle in which she moved. Her duties to the church and the poor claimed a part of her time. Then she was very fond of music, and kept up her own piano practice in a way not common with ladies of her age. Her children and friends accepted her new protegée unquestioningly. They learned from her scant revelations that the protegée was their peer in every womanly excellence; that she was without kindred this side the ocean, and that she was in need of just such a friend as Mrs. Rossington had chosen to become. That sufficed them.

"Miss Ludlow has the style of beauty that, whether in man or woman, always enslaved my mother." So said Mrs. Wheeler, the eldest daughter.

"My father had it, and Frank inherited it from him. It was the violet eyes, white skin, and gold-brown hair that made the telling appeal."

At first Mrs. Rossington gave her guest her exclusive attention. The change of location necessitated for Emily a new and suitable wardrobe, and her hostess interested herself in its preparation with true feminine zest. Emily's wonderful grace was a source of genuine pleassure to her new-found friend, who delighted to note the effect upon her of tasteful and modish attire. As days passed they became deeply and well acquainted; the elder woman acting always the part of enlightener as well as sympathizer. Notwithstanding all this kindness, and the congeniality of her new surroundings, Emily felt the old unrest coming back upon her strongly, with something added — a tinge of self-blame for what she hardly knew; possibly for certain stubborn crudities of disposition and consequent past action, for which, after all, she was not to blame.

Mrs. Kitzmiller had said to her, —

"Begin your new life as cheerfully and hopefully as possible. There is a place for you in the world — the right place. Keep your head level and your conscience clear, and your road to that place will be made plain."

She tried to remember the good woman's words and draw comfort from them; but, in spite of everything, a sense of want and isolation at times weighed her down. She belonged to no one; no one belonged to her. What if peril, sickness, or death should come? It would be hard to go down with no loving arms stretched wildly forth to hold her back! She thought of Truesdale; he had offered her much — too much to accept, unless she could show something more than this pale flame of gratitude in return.

At length he came, and she was glad. Still she would not grant the promise for which he begged; would scarcely grant enough of love's privilege to keep hope alive.

"What have you been doing all these endless days," he asked, "while I have been despatching matters with reckless haste to be with you?"

"Thinking," she replied; "thinking over all my past."

"Do not think of that, but of the future."

"No, I seem to think mainly of the past. I have been trying to make myself out; to make out some sort of estimate of that strange — I mean"—

She could not name Thorn, but Truesdale understood her, and said, with a smile,

"If seeing him almost daily for several years could not help you to that estimate, thinking about him now can hardly do so."

As days went by he grew puzzled over her complex uncertainty. She was not capricious; she was far too earnest for that. While she would give him no positive encouragement that she would ever become his wife, she always received him with a warm, quiet gladness that made him long for their hour of meeting. To himself he called her a beautiful mystery.

The winter weeks passed on, and Truesdale came and went. At length one day he returned to her after a two weeks' absence in New York, feeling a premonition that he would hear his final answer. He found Emily watching for him at the window, and it gave him a throb of buoyant confidence. She met him at the door, and, taking his offered hand, led him to the sofa. She even held his hand a little after they were seated.

"You have made an escape, my friend," were her first words.

"An escape!" he queried, in those mellow, deferential tones that went straight to the heart of every woman who heard them.

"Yes, I am going away, and I am glad to go. I have just received a letter from my mother's brother, urging me to come to Scotland. I found his address in looking through some old papers of my parents' that Mr. Wycoff gave me just before I came here. I wrote, and this is the answer."

"You look elated," he said.

"Yes, I feel a great relief. I am calm, and sure of everything now."

"You are sure you do not love me, and never could?"

"My willingness to leave you forever puts it

beyond doubt. And so I say you have made
an escape; for I might have been persuaded;
and marriage without love, or love only on one
side — death, you know, is to be preferred."

Truesdale rose suddenly and crossed the
room. He was strongly moved, and until he
had gained self-mastery he did not let her see
his face. He had not schooled himself for ulti-
mate failure, and it was very bitter. To miss
what his whole heart longed for — to find himself utterly baffled where he had dreamed con-
fidently of success! He was perhaps not vainer
than other men of great personal advantages,
but he had always enjoyed a happy sense of his
own power. And this woman, so lonely and
so sympathetic, had kindly and firmly put aside
his earnestly proffered love. With a free heart
she could not do it! So, in the sudden reaction
of his self-esteem, he declared. Yet what was
the secret of her preoccupation, if preoccupied
she was?

"When do you go?" he asked, returning to
her side.

"Perhaps in a month or two; Mrs. Rossington says not until June. But you must go at
once. It would have been better if you had

not come. You have stayed too long; but I have been so weak! I was flattered and soothed, and did not think I might be wronging you. My history has been one of mistakes —my own and others', and I am infinitely sorry."

A little later he said all there was left to be said —"Farewell!" and "God bless you!"

When Truesdale disappeared from New Madrid, the surmise was commonly expressed that he had "followed John Thorn's wife." The Kitzmillers felt sure of it. For a time Emily wrote weekly letters from Albany; then there fell a long silence, over which Olive grieved and wondered.

" She is goin' to be married," said Mrs. Kitzmiller, "and she do n't rightly know how to talk about it on paper."

That evening, about the time of winding the kitchen clock, she remarked to her quiet partner, —

"Well, it 's just as I expected, and as everybody else expected; but it don't seem right to me, and it don't to her, or she would n't have stopped writin'."

Her usually docile listener for once felt disposed to make reply.

"That's so, Lucy," he said; "there is a sort of wrong-seemin' about it. But it's something that's done all around us every day in the year. People get divorced, and marry somebody else, and settle down and get along right comfortable. In a good many cases they r'ally seem to have bettered their circumstances." The answer to this came sharp and sudden.

"Dan'l Kitzmiller, if there's the least mite of good reasonin' in that, I'd like to be made to see it! You know 's well 's I do that the whole State of Indiana's doin'. of it would n't make it right, if it was n't right afore!" Daniel, not being of an argumentative turn, made no response to this, and his better half talked on.

"It would be next to impossible to make me believe Emily was n't *all right;* but I'm not quite so sure about Truesdale. And if he is n't as honest a man as she is a woman, she'll be a sight more unhappy with him than she ever was with Thorn. If she could 'a' been rid out of the idea that John knew about the old man's money afore he married her, she could n't 'a' helped respectin' him; everybody else does. He's maybe a harsh, overbearin' sort of a man; but I believe his character's built on a solid foundation of good principle. I'm not so sure about Truesdale."

To Olive she said,

"Be patient awhile, dearie; one of these days you'll get a paper with her weddin' notice in it. Then you may write to her again, but I would n't now."

No such paper ever came to Olive, but at last a letter came, an earnest, loving letter, assuring her that she had not been forgotten for a single day or hour. In it Emily said,

"I am not married. I do not expect to be. I have opened my heart upon this subject to Mrs. Rossington as freely as I could. Some day she will tell you all. In June I expect to go to my relations in Scotland. I shall take with me your sweet picture, and the thought of your love and your dear mother's wonderful kindness as a priceless possession. I suppose you sometimes see Mr. Thorn. I hope the look of anxiety and discontent has gone out of his face. Surely life must seem brighter to him now that he is quite free; and when I have left this pitiless continent forever it will seem brighter yet. After I have sailed, you may tell him."

But Olive did not wait for Emily to sail. That evening she waylaid Thorn between his house and the tannery, and gave him the letter. He glanced at the envelope and grew pale.

"Is this for my eyes, Olive? Does she want me to read it?"

"*I* want you to read it, Mr. Thorn. She does not know what she wants, and never did!" She started to leave him; then the impulsive child turned, and taking the hand that held the letter in both her own, she said, —

"Oh, be good to her, Mr. Thorn, and bring her back! I cannot have her go so far away! You must not let her go! Please be good to her and bring her home!" Then, loosing his hand, she flitted away in the closing night.

Thorn read the letter by his counting-room lamp. The thin little sheets still fluttered in his trembling hand, when Davy Ransom gave the door a thump, and thrust in an arm, with the word "Mail." John took the letters. The first one his eyes fell upon was posted at Buffalo, and addressed in a handwriting as familiar to him as his own. He threw it down with a

muttered curse ; then tore it open and took in
the contents with one savage glance : —

"DEAR THORN, — Once you were audaciously honest
with me, under very peculiar circumstances; now it is
my turn. I have played high, and lost. Fate and a
woman's incomprehensible will were against me. I
have reason to believe that my defeat means your vic-
tory.   H. T."

CHAPTER XX.

WHEN Horace Truesdale found himself again *en route* for the West, he had no intention of taking New Madrid in his course. His two months' sojourn in his native State had shown him that the East could never again be home to him. He had learned to love Indiana, with its life-teeming forests, lakes, and marshes. His whole being had become saturated with their subtle aroma; his ear had grown quick for their peculiar sounds, — the call of the wild turkey, the whistle of the snipe, the drumming of the fan-tailed grouse. But Indiana was not the goal of his present journey. He had said to himself at starting, —

"Omaha certainly; Virginia City probably."

He reached Fort Wayne in the night. There would be a delay of some hours before he could go on to Chicago. He went to a hotel where he had often put up before, took a room, and retired to bed. He was within a long day's ride of his late home; he might never be so near again. He lay with closed eyes, thinking of

many things. The future was not without color
and attractiveness, notwithstanding he was a
recently disappointed man. He was full of
healthy enterprise; his zest for nature, and his
interest in the vast, wild region toward which
his steps were tending, were very great, though
a sincere and poignant regret rankled in his
heart. He thought of his schemes for the future; but his thoughts ever and again recurred
to New Madrid, his old den, and the good rifle
that lay in its hooks above the low door. He
recalled his pets, one by one. He had, before
he left, bestowed them upon various friends
and acquaintances. If it had been spring he
might have given them the freedom of the forest, but at that season it would have been cruelty to do so. Susie Hodges had adopted Sam
Slick at his particular request. He would like
to see Sam again. He greatly wanted that
gun; perhaps he would send for it some time.

He fell asleep and dreamed he saw Susie
walking with Charlie Walters, swinging his
hand in a childish way, their fingers locked
together. He thought, in his dream, he ought
to be in Charlie's place, for he had often walked
that way with her. Their backs were toward

him; but he called her name, and she turned quickly, revealing, not the face of his Black-eyed Susan,. but that of an aged and withered woman, with gray hair and sunken eyes. The change gave him a shock, but the instant her glance rested upon him the rich blood mounted to her cheeks and brow, a soft fire kindled in her dark eyes, and, loosing her hand from that of her companion, she clasped it with its fellow upon her breast, and stood before him a radiant, smiling image of youth and beauty.

It was snowing furiously when he went down to breakfast in the dimly-lighted dining-room. That meal being finished, he walked through the office to the street door and viewed the situation. An omnibus, with a lantern at its front, stood waiting to carry passengers to the westward-bound train. And there stood the heavy, lumbering old hack, with its black, flapping oil-cloths, that would reach New Madrid some hours after dark. He lighted a cigar and climbed into it,—the only passenger for that dismal day's ride. He wanted his rifle.

He dined at the Windfall, a half-way house kept by a man named Stots, who expressed much surprise at seeing him, and joked him

about "running away with the grass-widder."
He reached Rounce's about eight that evening,
exchanged brief greetings with its astonished
proprietor, and sat down to warm his chilled
feet, without removing his overcoat.

"Yes, I'll have supper presently, but I'll
step out first. I left a good rifle in my den
over yonder; am curious to see if it's there yet
all right."

"The place 'll be dark as a blackleg's heart,"
said Rounce.

"I've got matches." said the other, starting
out, "and there's a candle on the shelf."

As he approached the little square box that
had somehow been in his mind's eye all day, he
thought he saw a glimmer of light through a
crack in the closed board shutters. He turned
the knob of the door, found it unlocked, and
entered. A lantern, with a dimly burning
candle in it, stood in the middle of the bare
room, and at its farther side sat a woman or
girl, leaning forward, with her face resting upon
the table at which he used to write. She lifted
her head as he approached; it was Susie, or the
pale ghost of Susie! A murmur of compassion
escaped Truesdale's lips, and he involuntarily

opened his arms to the forlorn girl, who clung
to his breast sobbing, but with tearless eyes.
She trembled violently, and he knew that he
was supporting almost her entire weight upon
his arm. He sought her pulse and realized that
she was in danger of fainting. Replacing her
in the chair from which she had risen, he drew
forth a traveller's flask of brandy, and made
her taste it. As he held and chafed her hands,
he could feel all their little bones with startling
plainness. He passed his hand up over her arm
and shoulder, whence the pretty, girlish round-
ness had gone; over her face, with its sharp
outlines and sunken eyes.

"Great Heaven! Susie, can it be that you
have suffered like this for me! What brings
you here to-night so late?"

She could not find her voice, but answered in
a soft whisper, —

"I went to the store for some lining for father,
and just stopped in a moment as I was passing."

He glanced at the table and saw upon what
she had been pillowing her sad face — a pair of
his own leathern gauntlets, which he had care-
lessly left there. Drawing her head against
him, he said in tones of tenderest pity, —

"Poor little girl! I did not know; I never dreamed it was so deep a thing!"

"I never meant you should know," she sighed; "but now I do not care. I kept up well till after you were gone."

"Yes," he repeated, "you kept up well. You even encouraged Charlie Walters. He was with you a good deal just before I left."

He removed her shawl and replaced it with his own great-coat, warm from his person, using the shawl to wrap well her feet and ankles. Then he drew up another chair and seated himself beside her.

"I want to talk with you a little while, Susie, and this place is like Spitzbergen. Are you comfortable so?"

She answered with a long sigh, nestling closer in his arms.

"Do you know where I have been, Susie?"

She raised her head slowly, and looked at him earnestly for a moment.

"I had almost forgotten," she said. "You followed Emily Thorn. Are you married?"

"No," he replied, "and never will be to her. I wanted her, but she would n't have me. I received her final answer only a week ago. She rejected me firmly, though I begged hard."

"Poor Horace! if you have felt as I have," murmured the fond girl.

"I have not felt as you have, dear," he said, with a slight smile of self-disdain. "I'm afraid I could never feel like that. But I loved her, and wanted her. Now I am going to ask you to take what she refused. Did you ever hear of Omaha, Susie? I am going on there to-morrow. Will you be married to me in the morning, and go, too?"

"If I live till morning. If this happiness does not kill me. But wait," she said, looking up, with her deep, pathetic eyes. "I must tell you something first. You remember when Emily was thrown from her horse, and her arm broken. She said some girl threw herself before the horse and frightened him purposely. It was true, and it was I. I saw her coming as I sat by the roadside, and something made me do it. I think I wanted her to be killed: but I was miserably sorry afterwards. I did not mean it, but I could not help it. Something made me do it — something that quite mastered me for the moment. Can you forgive me? I think she would forgive me if she could understand."

"Poor Susie!" he said, stroking her rich, dark hair with great gentleness. "You were very wicked, but very wretched. I think she would forgive you if she could understand. I will take you home now. The clerk's office is still open, and I will procure the license to-night; to-morrow morning, before the stage goes out, you will be my wife. But think well, my child; you are giving up a good deal. Those bad little brothers of yours are very fond of you, and your parents will grieve to lose you."

"They were losing me anyhow," she said; "I could not have lived till the woods were green."

Again his boundless compassion, which was perhaps his predominant trait, prompted him to fold her in a closer embrace, as he said, "I haven't much to offer in return for your fresh, girlish tenderness, but I will be kind to you, and faithful."

The words were spoken not merely as a promise, but as a vow; and he kept it.

CHAPTER XXI.

THERE are crises in every life of strong and varied experience, which leave the individual in an attitude of vague expectancy. These pauses, when the soul looks Fate in the face with a question, are usually speedily rewarded. After Truesdale's departure Emily found herself in just this waiting, questioning mood. To Mrs. Rossington she one day said, —

"If I do not take passage for Scotland at once, I believe I will never go at all."

"And what if you do not?" said her friend. "I would be glad if you would willingly abandon the project, and begin to shape your life to the conditions around you now, as though this city were to be your future home."

"I feel sure it will not be," said Emily, though why she said it she could not tell. A moment later a wave of self-reproach swept over her, and she added quickly, —

"You have been a friend and mother to me, dear Mrs. Rossington, and everything is most

177

pleasant for me here, yet I feel sure this place
will not be my future home.   I do not say this
from any conscious choice, but from an unde-
fined yet strong impression."

There was a long silence between them, which
the elder lady broke by saying, —

"There is no day of my life that I do not
take blame to myself for not having supple-
mented the knowledge you voluntarily gave me
of your unhappy relations with Mr. Thorn, by
some further acquaintance with you both before
I left Indiana."

Emily put by, with a strong hand, the embarrassment which the mention of Thorn's name
always brought with it, and asked, —

"What would you have done if you had
known us better?"

"Perhaps I might have helped you to know
each other better.   At all events I would have
tried to convince you of what I now fully believe, that your husband was your devoted lover;
however you might have taken it."   Emily's
voice was very low as she said, —

"I *believe that now*, at least, and I take it like
all the rest, rather painfully."

One stormy evening, some two weeks later,

Mrs. Rossington opened her street door herself to admit a tall stranger, who asked in mellow, western tones for Mrs. Thorn. The widow was a shrewd woman, quick to think and to act. Giving him her hand in token of cordial welcome, she said, —

"You are Mr. John Thorn. Before I take you to Emily I have ten words to say and a question to ask."

He stood uncovered, holding the hand of the earnest, eloquent little lady in a close clasp, a look of concentrated interest and emotion suffusing his strong face. The words were said, the question asked and answered; and, with a joyous light on her face, Mrs. Rossington conducted him into the presence of the woman he sought, and closed the door upon them.

He went straight to her, but stopped within two paces.

"Emily!" he said; "my poor, pale love! Will you forgive me, and let me hold you to my heart?"

She threw up her arms — the signal of surrender — and let them fall around his neck.

How the snow fell during the days that followed! Emily will never forget that week; the steadily, noiselessly descending snow shower; the blank whiteness of the world without; the muffled sounds and shapeless figures in the street; the glowing coal-fire in the parlor grate; the sense of soft seclusion under the sheltering wings of the storm; the long hours of earnest talk or happy silence with John Thorn. For, though no one else came, the storm did not keep him away. One morning he found Emily writing. She rose suddenly and put away her papers.

"Did I interrupt you?" he said; "it is very early, I suppose, and — I have come too soon?"

"No," she answered, "I grew impatient to tell you something that I forgot yesterday; so I commenced writing it. I thought if something should prevent your coming to-day, and we never met again, you could read it."

"Why, what *could* prevent my coming," he asked wonderingly.

"Nothing, of course," she replied; "but I am always full of strange fancies,— whims if you choose. And all this seems so unreal. Each morning when I wake I wonder if it is not all a dream — your coming and loving me so, and — my happiness."

They were standing in the middle of the room. He had lifted her hands upon his breast, and held them there clasped under his own. Still standing thus he begged her to tell him the dear thing she had forgotten yesterday. So she took him back to that sad time when Frank Rossington lay a corpse at Kitzmiller's.

"That was one of the times when, for a little while, I forgot to be suspicious and afraid of you. You were so calm and helpful, yet so truly sympathetic. The tenderness of your nature showed itself in many little ways! Just then, if you had spoken gently to me, or laid your hand upon me, I could have clung to you and sobbed out all my loneliness and heartbreak, here on your breast!"

He took his breath with a short, strident sigh.

"And just then I spent long, sleepless nights, almost destroyed with the violence of the struggle between my great longing to offer you my love, and my fear of giving you deadly affront! Not more than once in centuries could such a history as ours be possible!"

Another day she begged leave to make a confession. It was that she had sometimes contrasted him unfavorably in her thoughts with others who were more fluent talkers. And that now his conversation was a constant surprise to her; his knowledge of and interest in things to which she had always supposed him to be indifferent.

"In short," said Thorn, "I have seemed to you only a money-maker. That mistake was the rock of our shipwreck. And it was a mistake. One of the few formulated principles of my philosophy is not to regard money as an end, only as a means. I have had my dreams of travel and self-improvement, of a life of restful activities very different from the one which I have lived. But the money had to be made. A man with a good intellect — such as, without vanity, I know I have — could hardly live my life of business and politics and be an ignoramus. He need not be a boor. And though I am not naturally bookish, I have read a good deal these last years. It has been a solacing act of devotion to you."

She glanced up with a smile whose confusing sweetness made him find his voice with an effort, when she repeated the whispered question, "How to me, John?"

"Why, I know you were always reading, and I managed generally to find out what. It is the only thing, dear, about which I ever spied upon you. I think you will find in my den in the currier's shop almost every volume you have read and thought about for three years."

"And we might have read and thought about them together!" she murmured.

At length the snow ceased to fall; and one afternoon a small bridal party entered the gray old church, the stones of whose walls were dear to Mrs. Rossington's heart. A few family friends of Mrs. Rossington were present. Emily appeared on the arm of a gray-haired brother of the widow, who gave her away in due form. Standing there in that mellow light, with the robed priest reading the quaint, impressive service of the Church, a quick vision crossed Emily's mind of that other bridal scene, — so long, so long ago it seemed! — the cabin in the woods; the palsied old man on the bed; the lame schoolmaster standing before them, not without a certain dignity of his own, — for a brief instant it was all vividly present. Then the organ sounded a glad, soft peal, and John and Emily Thorn walked forth into a new life together.

Emily remained with Mrs. Rossington until spring. Thorn returned almost immediately to Indiana. He wished to prepare his home for her coming. He wished also that their neighbors might be somewhat prepared.

In one of her long letters to Olive, Emily said, "I think so often of all our neighbors. I mean in future to know them better, and know them for their good and my own. It shall be the aim of my life to walk with them in ways of mutual helpfulness and kind judging. You and I, Olive, will do something for the girls we know. Their environments are so narrow, their aims so petty! If there are any among them who can be waked up to the fact that life is a lesson-day as well as a work-day and play-day, — waked up to habits of thought and observation, we will find them out. It will be a sort of *mission* for us."

Olive read this to her mother, who remarked dryly, "I don't like that use of the word mission. It belongs to religious work. And after all, folks need savin' more than civilizin'. It isn't every one that *can* be just so cultivated, but every one may have their sins forgiven."

Of course, during Emily's absence many

things were said that would have been painful
for her to hear. That which was uttered with
most contempt was, that John Thorn had taken
her back after Truesdale had deserted her. To
this Mrs. Kitzmiller, who attended quiltings
and other neighborhood gatherings with an assi-
duity she was never guilty of before nor afterwards, would reply, —

"Nobody in their senses, who knows John
Thorn, would believe that for a moment."

Owing to this good friend's steadfast cham-
pionship, supported by the fact that she knew
more of Emily's life after her departure from
the Wycoff settlement than any one else, the
tongue of curious and damaging gossip was at
length silenced; and when, in the early spring,
John brought her home, she was welcomed by
all with a cordiality warm and unfeigned.

As soon as was deemed proper she was waited
upon by a large visiting party, under the leader-
ship of Mrs. Kitzmiller. On this occasion no
embarrassing allusions were made, and these
somewhat narrow but well-meaning neighbors
preserved a degree of prudent reserve as sur-
prising as it was commendable.

They found Aunt Thirsa deposed from her

position of domestic autocrat, partly by rheumatism, partly by John's firm yet kind order that Emily should be mistress in everything.

She sat in her splint-bottomed rocking-chair, clean and cool, and kindly waited upon. Though not able to hear the lively chat about her, she seemed to enjoy it, and would occasionally break out and talk a little herself.

"I always expected to have to give up doin' things when John got married, and I'm proper glad it's Emily I got to give up to. She never had no nack o' housework, and the sight of a hired gal always did make me sick; but land knows I got no cause to complain s' long 's I'm 's well off as I am."

After dinner John showed the visitors the spot which he and Emily had selected for their new house, and together they displayed their drafts and plans for the house itself, receiving pleasantly suggestions so numerous and incongruous, that, if adopted, the structure must have proved one of the world's wonders.

The short spring afternoon was wearing away. Motherly Mrs. Kitzmiller drew Emily aside for a little whispered congratulation and counsel; then there was a lively bustle of bonneting and shawling and leave-taking. Olive had been helping Emily all day, arranging the table and waiting upon the guests. At the gate her mother missed her.

"Where's Ollie?" she called. "Come, daughter, we're going now."

"Let Olive stay all night, please," said Thorn, from the porch; "my wife wants her."

"All right, if they'll keep in out of the dew," was the cheery response, as the worthy dame hurried off to join old Mrs. Wycoff and the rest, all of whom were unanimous in declaring that they had spent a delightful day, and that matters with John Thorn's folks were, at last, about as they should be.